Clothed in Silk

Dr. Sharon Campbell-Phillips

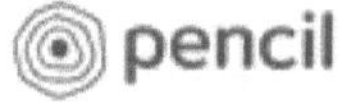

ISBN 978-93-5610-789-2
© Dr. Sharon Campbell-Phillips 2022
Published in India 2022 by Pencil

A brand of
One Point Six Technologies Pvt. Ltd.
123, Building J2, Shram Seva Premises,
Wadala Truck Terminal, Wadala (E)
Mumbai 400037, Maharashtra, INDIA
E connect@thepencilapp.com
W www.thepencilapp.com

Author biography

My name is Dr. Sharon Campbell-Phillips. I am from Trinidad and Tobago. I am very enthusiastic about community work and the development of others. I am also very passionate about conducting research and writing as it allows me the opportunity to share my knowledge with others and educate them as well as enhance and develop myself.

I am currently employed with the local government of Trinidad and Tobago where I work in the Division of Community Development. This Division is dedicated to developing communities so that persons' standard of living can be enhanced.

My writing career began when I was approached by a classmate from Bangladesh to collaborate and write professionally. I accepted the challenge and we began writing together. When I received my first publication, I was very excited and was motivated to continue writing, I am also a Doctor of Health Sciences. My passion for writing allows me to complete individual projects, as well as collaborate with others to produce impressive work.

Phone: +1868 7511022
Email: sharoncampbell433@gmail.com

CONTENTS

CHAPTER ONE

Thank God there has been a Starbucks across the road from the funeral home. At 7:00 that morning, Abra had taken the subway from her midtown Manhattan resort to Queens so she may want to discover an unobtrusive spot to examine the funeral. She was shaking considering she was given on the subway. The trembling becomes specifically substantive around her neck. She thought she seemed like a person with Parkinson's or Katherine Hepburn, in her old age whilst she shook like a leaf in a hurricane. But while she checked out her reflection within the subway window, she noticed that she wasn't shaking on the outside, only on the internal. As she gazed at her mirrored image within the glass, she began to ease. The rhythmic rocking of the subway soothed her.

It didn't truly rely on if someone noticed her sitting in Starbucks searching at the funeral domestic. No one could understand her. She was no longer the same Abra who became final in Queens sixteen years ago. She didn't even have the equal final call. Then she became Abra Ginzberg, now she become Abra Berg. She had chopped off the first half of her call the identical way she had chopped off the first half of her life.

She got off at the Queens Boulevard subway forestall and as she walked up the stairs to the street, she felt as if she have been growing from a grave. She pictured herself like a parent in a horror film - an obvious ghost in a white shroud wafting up from a coffin with hands outstretched and hair flying. She became getting back from her afterlife to her first existence.

Before she noticed the street, she felt it. With every step, her ears were bombarded with the sounds of visitors – buses moaning and groaning, motors beeping and screeching, people rushing up and down the steps speaking English with thick New York accents or babbling in incomprehensible tongues. The smells engulfed her. They permeated her pores and skin and have been absorbed using her cells. She felt that she might for all time reek of exhaust fuels and frying oils expelled into the road air from the restaurants. By the time she reached the top step, she become immersed in 1990, the final time she had walked those streets.

She headed the course of Goldstein & Simms Funeral Home. What a call for a funeral home, Jewish and WASP. In that manner nearly everyone was a capacity customer, something their religion. All they had to do became upload names like Hussain and Chang and they would cowl anyone. As she walked, she identified every inch of the street. She had spent a lot of her teenage years strolling these streets to do the family purchasing. Not looking for garments, tunes, or earrings, like different teenagers. No, looking for existence's requirements.

The funeral domestic changed three blocks from the house where she lived the primary eighteen years of her lifestyle. She stayed glued to Queens Boulevard not bold to undertaking everywhere close to Seventeenth Street. She didn't want to get a passing glimpse of the house or the street even though her own family now not lived there.

She searched the shops along the manner to discover people who had withstood time. There had been nevertheless the kosher butcher, candy shop, grocery, and cleaners. They regarded so small and dingy.

They probable had continually been small and dingy while she shopped in them, however, the sixteen years had reduced in size similarly and made them seedier and grayer. The grocery shop nonetheless had fruit displayed out the front. In 1990, she considered it old school and unsanitary, but now she thought it seemed nearly quaint. Like what you'll see on the streets of several of Europe's towns. Open-air fruit markets in London and Paris have been captivating. Open-air fruit markets in Queens with circling flies and grimy, germ-ladened arms pawing the products had been disgusting. What bacteria and lethal viruses had been transferred from one's fingers to the tomatoes? Years ago, whilst she had to shop for the product that changed into the simplest in outdoor packing containers, she dug to the bottom to find the fruit that have been least contaminated. After she was given home, she washed this produce as though she were an obsessive-compulsive washing her hands.

But now there were new shops. There was Barnes and Noble, Old Navy, and, of direction, the ever-gift Starbucks. There were all sorts of ethnic restaurants and even a halal marketplace to counterbalance the kosher butcher. She shifted her interest from the stores to the hordes of people on the street. She recalled that the streets had always been jammed irrespective of the time. In New York, humans looked like automatons, mainly early in the morning. The ones rushing to the subway looked like they had been wound uptight, like toy tops that start turning in perfect circles and steadily wobble until they fall. So many have been speaking on their cells, and still, others had been preserving the cells to their ears for security or their downloading of mind cancer waves. Who were they talking to so early in the morning? If you didn't see the telephones, you will think that they were the schizophrenics wandering the streets speaking to their demons. They sounded crazy because they spoke in loud voices as though they were yelling orders to underlings. Why did human beings have to scream once they were in cells? They didn't do this with landline phones. There have been only a few facial expressions visible on those early morning rushers – preoccupation, fear, anger, but never smiles or eagerness.

There had been girls buying in the vintage stores at this early hour. The vintage shops weren't like the new ones that opened at 10:00. The old ones opened early and stayed open late to accommodate folks that labored long hours and had long commutes and, of the route, to make extra cash. She noticed that a number of the shops had distinctive proprietors. In the sweet store, there have been now Asians in the region of the antique Jewish couple who had saved the shop open from 6:00 a.m. until the middle of the night. When had the ones humans slept? Where had they slept? They never made communique whilst Abra offered cigarettes for her mother or sweets for Rachel and Noah. They in no way regarded in her eyes even though she has been in the shop infinite times. They exuded anger and hate, now not for Abra, but for life, their lives.

Abra remembered her morning shopping journey at 7:00 earlier than she left for school. She had to make sure that there were sufficient meals for her mother and father at the same time as she become a faculty. She knew the vicinity of the whole lot within the grocery shop. She could find the soup cabinets with her eyes closed. She sold gallons of soup, in particular Campbell's hen noodle. Everyone cherished that alongside thick slabs of challah slathered with butter. Suddenly she realized that the

Jewish bakeries become long gone. Every day she bought challah and bagels and baileys. They never got stale because they were eaten three meals an afternoon. Where had the bakery been? She thought maybe that became what the Thai eating place turned into. What a trade – pad Thai for challah.

She additionally remembered the nighttime visits to the drugstore. She ought to be twelve when she began going to the pharmacy to get the medicinal drugs for something changed into incorrect with the children or her dad and mom. Wasn't she afraid to stroll the streets at night time even though they have been properly lit and full of people? She couldn't forget what she concept. She most effectively remembered her moves. She did what had to be performed and he or she didn't think about it. Now she turned reflective approximately every motion she took. Now she turned into alone – she wasn't liable for anyone however herself. Then she had the burden of the Ginzberg international on her shoulders, and what a heavy world that became. But she never consciously thought about it. From an early age, she knew she became chargeable for her entire own family, however, she usually knew she wouldn't be chained to them for her complete lifestyle. She knew she might make her terrific getaway.

She walked slowly and tested the women who rushed with her aid of her. Some were dressed for paintings and pushing children in strollers or conserving their fingers, in all likelihood taking them to daycare. These women appeared so harried, so frantic like the day had opened with hundreds of hours of factors for them to do within the next confining twenty-four hours. She questioned if she had looked like that after she went off for her morning buying. Rachel and Noah didn't visit daycare. When they weren't in school, Abra become their toddler sitter. Even if daycare had been available, no person could have taken such broken children. She turned into even her dad and mom's infant sitter. It changed into a disgrace there was no discern daycare in which she could depart them. Oh, how she needed respite from her no-way-ending duties.

The community had changed over the past sixteen years, however, it additionally hadn't been modified. There had been nonetheless lots of Jews, however, they have been extraordinary now. There have been lots of old Jews. The younger ones had moved to the suburbs or the exurbs for special geography, one with distance among people. In Queens, human beings have been squashed together in their residences, on the streets, and in the shops. There turned into no greenery. Everything becomes grey and urban. The more youthful Jews had opted for the area, greenery, and the proverbial white wood fence. Now, there were also overseas Jews, especially Russians, on the first forestall earlier than they, too, moved on searching for area and greenery. To upload spice to the community, there were some non-Jews from all parts of the Arab international, Asia, and Latin America. This old Jewish community of New York was dissolving.

Abra knew diversity first hand. She worked for the Fairfax County faculties in Virginia, one of the most diverse faculty systems within the United States. There had been kids from loads of nations speaking a babel of languages. She had to test and counsel youngsters who spoke Urdu, Kurdish, Tagalog, and languages no one had heard before the children arrived on the faculty's doorstep. But Fairfax County's diversity wasn't the same as Queens's range. Fairfax had begun with a small white WASP populace, whilst Queens had started with a massive populace of Jews, a few American-born, and others from European international locations. There had never been a "real American WASP" in Abra's Queens.

Although she labored in a multicultural melting pot, Abra lived in an enclave of in most cases prosperous American-born whites. Her lifestyle turned into like a small island of white bread floating in a massive ocean of humus. Her pals have been broadly speaking white, with a sprinkling of Asians, all American born, all well-knowledgeable, and call center class.

She turned amazed that she remembered the stores so vividly. She even recalled some of the large cracks on the sidewalk. She had constantly walked together with her head down determined to carry out her missions and cautious not to trip on the jagged portions of concrete sticking up. She made thousands of trips to the grocery, pharmacy, and exclusive government offices. She became the lifeline to the outside global for the folks who lived in condominium 2D at 4313 17 Street. She became the authentic consultant who spoke to the sector on behalf of the Ginzberg family. She made cellphone calls and crammed out forms. She was even the only one who did the banking. From an early age, she knew how to deposit the authorities' incapacity tests that supported them. She started out writing assessments for lease, energy, and cellphone when she became ten. Using her satisfactory penmanship she finished every segment and then had her father sign on the signature line. He wrote like an infant with large, shaky letters bunched together. Jacob A. Ginzberg. A for Aaron. Everyone within the family had biblical names, although no person study the Bible or went to synagogue.

Today Abra labored with children who acted on behalf of their mother and father managing the demands of residing and running in an overseas tradition. These children were like UN translators as they ably spoke English to doctors, attorneys, policemen, and landlords, and translated lower back into their dad and mom's tongue. But it become specific from what she had carried out. The mother and father of those youngsters generally made the selections, and the youngsters were the best translators. Abra had to make decisions for folks that didn't have the intellectual capability to achieve this. Her dad and mom had grown up within the culture, however, hadn't absorbed it. They had been in adults' children's bodies.

She entered Starbucks and ordered her normal Grande thin latte. As she seemed round, she once more showed that Starbucks became the equalizer for all cultural groups. There were Hispanic production people, Asians in business suits, and blacks with government ID tags around their necks. All had been shopping for unusual coffees that had been alien to their cultures they were alien to all of the US' subcultures. These had been coffees that had been created to unite all Americans, and now all coffee customers of the world. People of all international locations cherished caramel macchiato, although no person knew what it become.

She picked up a far-read New York Post and settled on a stool at a window counter going through the funeral home. She looked at the paper and idea about the day before this. Was it most effective the day before this that she had seen the newspaper article about Rachel's drowning? An image on the front web page of a New York tabloid was how Abra learned that her sister died. That picture pulled her lower back sixteen years to an area she by no means desired to revisit. She became at National Airport on her manner to Charleston for an expert development workshop on computerized evaluation of ADHD and OCD. As she reached for a USA Today, her eyes were interested in the photograph and headline of the adjoining New York Post. The headline "Retarded lady drowns in the park lake," was plastered over a photograph of Rachel. How did she comprehend it turned into her sister? She hadn't visible her in sixteen years. She knew. She simply knew. She knew even before she read the item.

She bought the paper and discovered an empty gate. She sat facing the field so no one ought to see her face or her rapt hobby in what she changed into studying. Her eyes skimmed the item in a second and then went lower back and devoured it phrase by way of word, punctuation mark via punctuation mark. Her face changed so close to the paper that her nose almost touched Rachel's image.

On the front page became Rachel's faculty photograph while she changed into about sixteen. Inside, there had been images of the lake and the front of the organization home where Rachel lived. The text changed to brief. Rachel Ginzberg, a thirty-two-year-old woman with moderate intellectual retardation, drowned in the lake at

Hillside Park the day past. Ginzberg becomes a resident of the Oak Valley Home for Adults, a collection domestic for adults with disabilities. She became on an outing with five different residents of the house and three counselors. She had become separated from the group at the same time as taking a stroll. When the counselors found out that she was missing, they referred 911 and looked for her. An hour later, police located her inside the lake. A jogger, who refused to offer his name, recalled seeing her strolling through the park crying hysterically. He concept she was screaming "A-B" time and again. The counselors refused to be interviewed. Research into the incident is pending.

A-B. Abra tried to train Rachel to read some of the letters of the alphabet, however, she ought to most effectively consider A-B. Sometimes she referred to as Abra A-B, generally whilst she wanted Abra to study with her. She cherished whilst Abra read books to her, specific books about baby animals. They might each make the sounds of a kitten, a puppy, and a duckling. Abra stated meow. Rachel said something like meow. Abra said Arf. Rachel stated something like Arf. Abra said quack. Rachel said something like a quack. Those books constantly calmed Rachel whilst she turned agitated and nothing else worked. The sight of Abra taking away her books, particularly the child animal books at once sedated Rachel. She could have been an exquisite reader had she been born with one hundred extra IQ points.

Why had she known as out for Abra in her final moments? Did she nonetheless recollect Abra after sixteen years? Did she suppose that Abra could by hook or by crook materialize from at the back of the trees and convey her off to safety? Why had she long passed into the lake? She didn't even like to take a bathtub so why had she long passed right into a huge tub? What went via that poor lost toddler's head those remaining minutes of her existence? How did she get into the deep water within the lake? When Abra concept of Rachel's hysteria and frantic searching, she was weakened with emotions of pity. She endured reading. Ginzberg is survived by way of her parents, Jacob and Miriam Ginzberg of 3457 Sea view Rd in Brooklyn, and a brother, Noah, thirty-one, of the Wakefield Home for Adults in Queens. The funeral may be held at the Goldstein and Simms Funeral Home in Queens on

Thursday. No point out of Abra. Her dad and mom didn't even consider adding her call. She turned into now not a part of Ginzberg's own family. She shouldn't have been surprised. She deserted them sixteen years in the past, and they commonplace it. They had no choice. What did they think of Abra after all these years? Did they place her out in their minds simply as Abra had positioned them out of her thoughts?

After analyzing the item in numerous instances, she knew that she had to go to New York. She needed to have some closure on what took place. She had located her family in an isolation chamber in her mind. Weeks might cross by without Abra ever considering them. But now, she needed to realize what had happened to her circle of relatives over the past sixteen years. Her thoughts went into action mode as she mentally listed all of the matters she had to do within the next few minutes. This is what she did nice — prepare, systematize, prioritize. First, she called Beth, her college roommate, who was also attending the Charleston meeting. She wasn't answering her mobile so she was probable with a customer. She left a message pronouncing that something had arisen and that she might be arriving on Thursday, in preference to Wednesday. She told her that they could nonetheless have time to stay up overdue and speak as they downed glass after glass of pinot grigio. Beth changed into Abra's closest pal even though they simplest noticed each different at expert meetings and on a few vacations. Their friendship dated again to the primary day of university once they were randomly paired as roommates. Beth, too, had selected a career as a psychologist. She changed into married and had twelve months old sons. Even though she and Abra loved every different dearly, Beth didn't have a great deal of time for Abra. Her life focused on her paintings and circle of relatives. Abra's existence targeted around her work and retaining vigil over her buried reminiscences.

Abra went to the United States Air gate and modified her ticket for a Thursday afternoon flight from New York to Charleston. The changes might price a fortune, but she couldn't consider cash proper now. Then she went to the United States Air go back and forth gate and bought a ticket for the subsequent plane to La Guardia. She called the Marriott in midtown Manhattan in which she had occasionally stayed when she attended professional meetings in the past and made a reservation for that nighttime at a fee that could have made Shylock shout "usury." Then she called the Charleston Marriott to cancel her Wednesday nighttime stay.

On the travel, she closed her thoughts to all of the recollections that had been trying to escape from the isolation chamber wherein they have been quarantined. She took out her e-book of New York Times crossword puzzles and solved page after page at a quicker than a common clip. She shut out her environment and focused on the pages of black and white squares. She became trying to fight off the pix of the past that have been seeking to invade her focus. She knew that the snapshots continually fluttered around her subconscious, but she labored difficulty at retaining them on the outskirts of immediate focus. She smiled faintly whilst she needed to provide you with a nine-letter phrase for AWOL: d-e-s-e-r-t-i-o-n.

When she arrived in New York, she took the trip to midtown after which a cab to her resort. She loved staying at the midtown Marriott due to its place. Being inside the middle of the bustle of the town made it possible for her to walk out of the inn and stand inside the center of Times Square underneath the shimmering pix projected on the bordering buildings. The whole globe was pictured on those symptoms – the Lion King, Smirnov vodka, and Calvin Klein underwear. She specifically loved nights in Times Square – there was no darkness, simply vibrant, pulsating lighting. In this experience, she wouldn't get a chance to walk right down to the village and sit down in Washington Square. Nor might she be able to walk to Central Park and spot the zoo as a grownup, something she had by no means carried out as a child. She became going to Queens. That wasn't New York City; that became hell. Although she had been to the metropolis normally over the last sixteen years, she had never considered crossing the river to Queens. To her, Queens become a long way from Manhattan as Australia.

When she was given to her room, she checked her laptop for the deal with and get in touch with the range of the funeral domestic. She is known for specifics approximately the funeral. It changed to ten o'clock on Thursday. Then she checked the convention software. She would only omit the opening dinner and keynote speaker. She may want to nonetheless get the two days of training that she needed for certification to apply for the assessments. She had planned to get to the convention a day early so that she should visit the college wherein she had interned eight years earlier. She became satisfied that she changed to flying home on Sunday. At least, that would deliver her time to peer her friends, the Nelsons, and stroll through the charming streets of Charleston. She would transport herself to different times... From the days of the Civil War and the Revolution. She would hear Porgy and Bess making a song or the guns of Fort Sumter introducing the Civil War. This became a great city for Abra to forget the right here-and-now and delivery herself to the past, to romanticized instances that have been made real for her in books and films. She expected herself in a ring skirt keeping a parasol as she strolled the cobblestone streets. Sometimes her get dressed and parasol had been a shiny blue, now and then a vivid yellow. Her blond hair became in ringlets including through a bonnet. Her complete face was covered with freckles and her lips glowing with a mild coating of red lipstick. Smiling coyly up at Rhett Butler and fluttering her faded blue eyes. Yeah – positive. Jewish Abra Berg took walks in a ring skirt in Charleston in 1860.

She truly wasn't sporting a ring skirt now. She became geared up in an expert uniform of a beige linen pant match with a white silk shirt and three-inch spiked taupe sandals. Her rings turned restricted to a gold chain around her neck and pearl studs in her ears. No blond ringlets for her. Her jet black instantly hair regarded love it had been ironed.

Since the age of eighteen, she had worn the identical hair fashion, reducing shoulder period immediately across. She wore the Veronica Lake appearance with the hair falling over her left eye, while she became at paintings and used a barrette to hold her hair in the back of her ear. Her black eyes appeared even blacker because the whites of her eyes appeared bleached without a tinge of grey or pink. To accentuate her huge black eyes and lengthy lashes, she used a black liner on her higher and decrease lids and thick mascara. The whites of her huge eyes and the brilliant pink lipstick she wore gave her a shiny Technicolor look. She never had freckles, no longer along with her darkish complexion. When she tanned, she was regarded as the many immigrants of color from all points of the globe. She didn't have a spherical face. She had the Ginzberg long horse face. She, Rachel, and Noah all had long horse faces, like Jacob. They appeared like they have been associated with English royalty with their international-renown horse faces. The Ginzbergs and their cousin, Prince Charles.

And she really wouldn't be looking up at Rhett Butler because along with her three-inch heels, she becomes five feet, ten inches. She probable could be taller than Clark Gable, the authentic Rhett Butler. He would have to coyly look up to her or she ought to painfully bend her knees to shorten herself. She emptied her latte and seemed via nowadays' Post for greater statistics on the drowning. The paper was full of photos of the previous day's gangland killing of a Mafia boss in Little Italy. The drowning became old news, actually and figuratively. There became not a lot to examine within the paper so she found a New York Times. For a couple of minutes, she turned into absorbed with the aid of articles on what changed going on in the international…famines in Africa, coups in Asia, and melting icebergs in Antarctica. Why do they name it information, whilst there has been nothing new approximately these statistics? It was the identical antique stuff. They must name it the olds, no longer the news.

At approximately 9:45 a black stretch limo pulled up at the doorway of the funeral domestic. The funeral home employee ants rushed out to open the limo door. They looked like insects in their black fits and white shirts and their fluttery, obsequious movements. She had continually wondered what sort of character loved working in the funeral domestic commercial enterprise. How did they address the endless grief of each person they encountered? Were those people like other professionals – did they make jokes approximately their customers? And who became their clients – the lifeless or the survivors?

She stuck fleeting visions of her circle of relatives as they exited the limo. She tried to take mental pictures of them, but everything turned going on too rapidly. She couldn't stop them in time. First out turned into her father. He changed into as large as ever, but now his hair became all grey. He became stooped over and looked like a puppet whose master had forgotten to tug up the strings making the puppet flop around. He didn't seem like he become six feet, three inches. Next was her mother, blanketed with a black veil making her invisible. Abra couldn't inform me if she had changed. A worker ant delivered a wheelchair for her and rapidly drove her via the front door. Then came her brother, Noah. He had placed on weight. She remembered him as a skinny, pimply-faced kid. She couldn't see his face truly so she didn't recognize if he became still pimply. An older woman was given out after

Noah. She took his arm and assertively guided him in. She has to be an aide or a nurse who became there to help Noah deal with the incomprehensible. His sister, Rachel, had died. His sister, Abra, had died sixteen years earlier, and now he had no siblings. Although Abra had most effective fleeting impressions of Jacob, Miriam, and Noah, she knew who they have been. She had spent twelve months a year for eighteen years understanding them.

They survived these final sixteen years without her. Somehow they were capable of finding someone to store and cook and pay the payments. They didn't die without her. Rachel died, however no longer due to the fact Abra left. She died due to the fact she become a nervous thirty-two-year-old with the intelligence of a four-year vintage. The antique got lost and panicked. The four-year-old fell into the lake and drowned due to the fact she couldn't swim. The twelve months old didn't die due to the fact Abra wasn't there even though she was referred to by her name. Abra had to maintain repeating that to herself to ensure there had been no doubts creeping into her mind. She had to ensure that she didn't feel any tinges of guilt about Rachel's loss of life. Even if she hadn't left the circle of relatives, she wouldn't have been able to keep Rachel. She saved repeating that to herself like a Zen mantra. "I couldn't have saved Rachel. I couldn't have saved Rachel. I couldn't have stored Rachel."

She became conscious that she wasn't the simplest person who had come early to observe the funeral. The paparazzi had been there. She hadn't noticed them in the beginning due to the fact she was focused on the circle of relatives. There had been so a lot of them. They snapped one photo after some other as each member of the family become rushed from the limo to the funeral home. Fortunately, they have been kept returned by way of boundaries. Otherwise, they could be in their own family's faces. The Ginzberg family was getting their fifteen minutes of fame. Tomorrow, she could see those pics on the front pages of all of the New York papers regardless of what number of Mafia killings there have been. New Yorkers, like anybody else, cherished peer grief. There has been even some TV reporters status in front of a barricade with the funeral home inside the historical past. Fortunately, they couldn't get near and thrust microphones within the grieving own family's faces and ask "How do you sense?" That had to be the stupidest question in the world. "How do you suspect we sense after losing a daughter?" But this became just some other way our society basks within the grief of others. Maybe it changed into a superstitious way of saying "If this horrible thing befell this character, it happen to me."

Abra watched as the mourners entered the funeral domestic. Who has been a majority of these people? She became positive that maximum had been here due to the notoriety of the case. There were few surviving relatives. Abra's paternal grandparents were useless. She didn't recognize approximately her maternal grandparents. There have been many professionals, likely from the social offerings businesses and group homes that ruled Rachel's lifestyle. There had been probable lawyers too, eager to sue the group domestic and the metropolis for negligence. Maybe, at final, the Ginzberg family could get wealthy. They would get wealthy by way of the latest, maximum stylish method – wealth by way of a lawsuit.

Abra couldn't hold sitting in Starbucks. Even though no

person became watching her, she felt restless. She left and walked to a Barnes and Noble down the street. She leafed thru the great sellers without seeing any phrases. She went to the psychology segment to peer what the charlatans had been telling the masses about having "good psyches" and a way to raise "Garrison Keillor children who were all above common." She didn't have trouble looking through any of the books. She knew the glib advice that poured from TV talk shows and self-assist books. She regularly had to deal with dad and mom who would undertake her by way of pronouncing "But Dr. Phil says…"

She walked back to Starbucks and waited for her own family to emerge. Slightly before 11:00, a hearse got here from around the again of the funeral home. The circle of relatives' limo covered up at the back of it. The funeral domestic ants whisked every family member into the limo as quickly as they had been whisked in an hour in advance. The paparazzi snapped their images once more. The TV newshounds gave their on-the-spot coverage of nothing. The mourners streamed out and were given into cars within the adjoining parking lot. Abra didn't wait for the procession to depart. There changed into nothing more for her to look at. What she witnessed showed that her family had survived without her. She walked to the subway station and took an educated return to Manhattan. She went to her resort to accumulate her suitcase and took a cab to LaGuardia to seize her flight to Charleston. She vowed to by no means once more see any of her circle of relatives. She vowed to by no means once more see Queens. This become a short-term drop-in that she could by no means repeat. She couldn't. The ache in her soul became searing, threatening to interrupt via the metal armor she had painstakingly built over the past sixteen years.

CHAPTER TWO

After a day that appeared like a lifetime, Abra was given to Charleston at approximately 10:00. She had to trade planes in Charlotte, and as traditional, there was a delay. When she got off the plane in Charleston, she at once felt converted. The warmth and humidity of the September nighttime told her that she had clicked her sparkly crimson shoes and left Oz and now she changed into Kansas. Well, not exactly Kansas, in particular in case you listened to the Southern drawls of the humans around her. She felt her body loosen up and her facial muscular tissues lighten.

She precious the twelve months that she spent across the river in Wando County serving her college psych internship. When she finished, she could have stayed to work, however, she wanted cash and South Carolina colleges had been notorious for upholding their Civil War past and paying slave wages. So she opted to work in wealthy Fairfax County, Virginia.

She was given a cab and went to the resort. Fortunately, it become darkish and he or she didn't should see the belt of poverty and rot surrounding the lovely historic middle of the metropolis. She continually felt like ultimate her eyes when she drove outdoor of the metropolis middle. She didn't need to see the clusters of black guys idly status round ingesting booze from paper baggage, the scrawny children walking without a destination, nor the rotting buildings with peeling paint and boarded-up home windows. She simply desired to peer at the restored homes, the upscale, over-priced stores, the aromatic restaurants with their southern cooking, and the state-of-the-art, properly dressed strollers. She didn't want to mar her fantasies of Revolutionary or Civil War Charleston with the realities of slavery, racism, and poverty. Charleston was like her lifestyle; it had the unpleasant component like Abra's first eighteen years and it had the adorable part like Abra's ultimate sixteen years.

When she got to the hotel, she checked in and was given the second key to the room that she and Beth were sharing. They had been in room 234. She laughed aloud. That changed into their dorm room range at Lee Hall in college. She couldn't trust that Beth have been capable of getting that room. It couldn't be dangerous. Abra knocked lightly due to the fact she wasn't positive if Beth become sound asleep. Being away from the needs of a twelve months old changed into a welcomed respite for Beth so she was in all likelihood sound asleep or analyzing.

"Is which you Abra?" Beth croaked sleepily. Abra observed with a "Yep." The ever-careful Beth looked through the peephole, unhooked the chain, opened the door, and hugged Abra tightly. It was nearly a year considering that they had remained visible every other, even though they have been almost every day touched by using email or cell phone. Standing before Abra was a sleepy model of the equal Beth from 1990. She never modified inner or out. She had an equal sturdy athletic build despite birthing a child and her refusal to do exercise which she notion changed into a waste of time. She became physically strong, and it was confirmed. She seemed like an 1800s farm wife who may want to without difficulty bale hay, build fences, and convey two buckets of water from the nicely. Beth had continually been plain on the outdoor. She wore little make-up; her thick mild brown hair turned into reduce short in a shag; and she or he wore cleanable, durable garments from J.C. Penny. She hated ironing so her garments had a slept-in appearance. Wrinkled apparel on a few people become elegant, but on Beth, it was just simple wrinkled. But when Beth checked out you, the interior came out. She had an excessive stare that appeared to mention, "Communicate with me. Share with me. I want to recognize you." Then there have been her eyes, which continuously twinkled, giving her the advent of constantly laughing. And whilst she did snigger, her eyes almost disappeared.

Beth became a congenital nurturer. She turned into a born to care approximately others. She unselfishly loved her husband, Tom, and their son, Clay. She loved all of the human beings she labored with at her job as a psychologist in a network mental fitness corporation. And, of direction, she loved Abra from the first day they met at Jackson College. Abra didn't understand the source of Beth's wellspring of loving-kindness, but she became so grateful that she turned into a recipient of it. Beth helped to make Abra into the individual she had become by using introducing her to a happy, lovely global and displaying to her how to stay in it readily. But even Beth didn't know approximately Abra's past. Now changed into time for show-and-tell. Abra needed to inform her about the first 18 years of her existence and surrender the lie that she had no family, besides Miss Benjamin.

Beth stated, "I am so worn out, I can't even speak. I

simply need to sleep. Clay becomes up ill all final night so I am exhausted. We'll communicate each second whilst we're not soaking up high-quality knowledge. I love you. Damn, you continually appear gorgeous, even in the dark after journeying all day." They kissed and Beth jumped returned to bed and straight away fell lower back asleep. Abra leisurely unpacked and thought returned to August 22nd, 1990. Abra was certainly blessed when she turned paired with Beth. God, or destiny, had despatched Beth to manual Abra in her new existence. She could fantastically consider every second of that first day when she arrived at university with Miss Benjamin. They had driven the seven hours from New York to Jackson College inside the lovable town of Linz in the middle of the ancient Shenandoah Valley of Virginia. Arriving at Jackson College changed into like touchdown on a spaceship on Mars and being greeted by pumpkin-headed inexperienced extraterrestrial beings.

The day started in sticky, cramped Queens and ended in tranquil, bucolic Linz. Miss Benjamin had picked Abra up at 7:00 AM and loaded into her vehicle the three suitcases that contained all of the property that Abra carried into her new existence. Eighteen years of existence packed into those three suitcases.

Abra waited so Miss Benjamin didn't see Abra say goodbye to her circle of relatives. She didn't see the hysteria, she didn't listen to the screaming and sobbing, and she didn't feel the wrenching ache of the separation. She didn't witness the wire being cut; she didn't see Abra open the apartment door with a black and white global on one facet and enter a Technicolor international on the alternative side, similar to the Wizard of Oz. After they'd pushed a while, Miss Benjamin gingerly tried to provoke a verbal exchange about Abra's departure. "I comprehend it becomes difficult leaving the circle of relatives. Did your bubbe and Zayda help out?" Abra turned her face to the side window and said, "Oh Miss B., I don't need to talk approximately it now or ever." Her voice dripped with disappointment. Miss Benjamin, in her ever-supportive way, stated, "I understand. We'll communicate approximately it at some point whilst you're prepared." Looking at her mirrored image in the window, Abra spoke back, "I'll in no way be geared up. I just want to bury my life up until an hour in the past right into a bottomless grave."

Abra left her own family that day in August and never went back bodily, however she went returned mentally thousands of instances. She would in no way forget her grandmother protecting Rachel on her lap and her grandfather clasping his palms around Noah's chest as she picked up her suitcases and fled. Despite being severely retarded, Rachel and Noah understood what became occurring. They knew that Abra turned into leaving all the time. They sensed that their lifeline became disappearing, leaving them to drown. Abra wouldn't be there to consolation them during the nighttime once they had nightmares of demons created by way of their stunted imaginations. Abra wouldn't be there to smooth them when they vomited or had diarrhea. Abra wouldn't be there to calm them with quiet songs when they had been trembling with agitation or worry. They wouldn't pay attention to incomprehensible phrases from world history and Spanish high faculty textbooks studied via Abra as she did her homework while looking after them. Abra wouldn't be there to keep them in her palms when the sector was cruel to them. They wouldn't be caressed via Abra as she lightly gave them lengthy, soothing strokes and despatched the message that they were precious humans even though God forgot to offer them their full ration of brainpower.

Abra had selected Jackson College because of Miss Benjamin, her freshman English instructor. Miss Benjamin was to Jackson for a conference on English ladies thriller writers. She thought it became the most ideal school for Abra, in contrast to Barnard College where she had gone. Barnard in Manhattan turned into too close to Queens. Jackson's picturesque campus becomes nestled in a small town masses of miles away in Virginia. When she turned into the convention at Jackson, Miss Benjamin became friendly with the pinnacle of the English branch, Emily Weaver. They shared ardor for English mystery writers, especially Ruth Rendell and P. D. James. After the convention, they communicated regularly and Emily visited Miss Benjamin as soon as she turned into New York. So whilst Abra and Miss Benjamin have been doing university planning for Abra, Jackson came up as an option. It wasn't college planning, it become planning a wreck from the jail that Abra had been locked in for eighteen years.

Abra become ranked twentieth in a category of five hundred, had SAT ratings of 1480, and changed into financially needy so she changed into a top candidate for a scholarship. Jackson was upgrading the instructional fame of its scholar frame because it had such a lot of legacies, students whose own families had attended Jackson over the years, however, have been mediocre, unmotivated students. They also desired a more diverse scholar frame, and a Jewish pupil from New York City could add range since a maximum of the students were Christians from the Mid-Atlantic States. Jackson healthy their mutual desires. For Abra, it was away from New York City and her own family and a place to re-invent herself. For Jackson, it turned into an excessive attaining of diverse pupils.

Abra had by no means visited Jackson earlier than August 22nd. She couldn't escape from her family for a few days so she applied through the mail and interviewed by way of phone and videotape. When they drove onto the campus, Abra couldn't trap her breath. This changed into her dream come actual. An idyllic university campus with college students mendacity in the grass analyzing books and chatting or leisurely taking walks on the paths, no longer on the grass. Everyone was white and well-dressed. There have been no crowds. There was no noise. There have been no raised voices. There had been no smells of fried meals and bus diesel. There turned into grass, now not grass, however acres and acres of lawn. It wasn't grass like a park, it became grass just like the Earth's skin.

When they arrived at Jackson, they drove to Lee Hall, Abra's new home. The dorm seemed majestic to her. The gray stone outdoors and the white columns looked like a movie set plantation. There had been even white rockers on the porch. As they climbed the steps, they have been greeted by way of a freshman guide with a yellow smiley face name tag with Laura ornately scripted on it. She was a pretty, blond sophomore from Richmond who spoke with a drawl and exuded Southern appeal from every pore. She changed into wearing a pink sleeveless top and plaid shorts and wore white shoes without socks. Around her neck, she wore a thin gold chain, and in her ears were pearl studs. Abra studied her garb. Someday she desired to look similar to her. Now she became carrying a navy polo shirt, jeans, and sneakers with thick athletic socks. Her mind told her that she continually needed to put on socks so her feet wouldn't sweat. And she wore her handiest rings, gold hoops that Miss Benjamin had given her for graduation. The high faculty commencement ring that her grandparents sold her became left in Queens together with the high faculty yearbook documenting Abra's accomplishments.

Laura grew to become a way to greet another freshman and her mother and father. Abra didn't look at the lady, she tested the parents. They had been so attractive and exuberant. They shared their daughter's exhilaration of going to university. The father was sporting a red polo shirt and plaid shorts, a plaid similar to Laura's shorts. Abra had never seen a man put on crimson earlier than. She couldn't consider any male on seventeenth Street carrying red. It might be like a declaration that he become homosexual. The mom became carrying mauve Capri pants and a matching pinnacle. Abra looked at Miss Benjamin. She changed into brief, maybe five feet, one inch, and stout. The words fireplace hydrant always came to mind whilst she looked at Miss Benjamin's determination. She turned into sporting a denim skirt with a vibrant flowered shirt in conjunction with her wedges. But what made Miss Benjamin so extraordinary from their mother and father become her face. Her face changed into pudgy and she had jowls that moved whenever she did. She had brown spots randomly splattered on her cheeks. Her black eyes have been buried at the back of thick frameless glasses. She appeared so foreign whilst as compared to the humans around her. Not foreign like a foreign us of a, however foreign like a distinctive lifestyle. She without a doubt regarded as Jewish. But as Abra looked at Miss Benjamin, she noticed that she was completely cushy with herself. She smiled warmly at each person. She didn't understand she changed into foreign. She felt that she was in shape anywhere she turned. She probably thought that she became appealing and stylish. What a female! Abra hoped that at some point she might sense as cushty with herself as Miss Benjamin.

"Hi, y'all. I'm Laura. Welcome to Jackson and welcome to Lee Hall, your property far away from domestic." Abra was afraid to talk. Her vocal cords have been frozen. Her New York accessory sounded coarse next to Laura's accessory. Laura had a high-pitched, female voice whilst Abra had a deep, almost masculine voice. "Hi Laura, I'm Abra Ginzberg. I'm so satisfied to be right here." Abra, who at Knox High School became the commander of the English language appeared like an aphasic groping for the proper words. Before Laura could act on the belief that Miss Benjamin became Abra's mom, Miss Benjamin interjected, "Hi Laura. I'm Edith Benjamin, Abra's cousin. I drove her down and I'll be supporting her get settled."

Laura every day this clarification as though it were normal for a person aside from parents to deliver a freshman to campus, in particular at an antique Southern school like Jackson. Laura consulted the listing on her clipboard and said that Abra would be in room 234 with Beth King. Abra already knew her roommate's name. During the summertime, she received a letter from the housing workplace with Beth's call, address, and phone wide variety. When Abra phoned, Beth's mom told her that Beth changed to spending the summer in England and wouldn't be lower back till some days earlier than college commenced. Abra changed into anxious about assembly Beth. She imagined that she might be splendid and sophisticated. She knew that Beth might observe Abra with unhappiness. She was unfortunate enough to be stuck with a Jew from New York who turned into simply a rube with no tradition. She could in all likelihood ask to be moved to any other room so that she may want to have a higher roommate. Laura stated that Beth had arrived earlier in the day. She gave Abra directions to the room. "Abra honey, I'm sorry I can't take you to the room, however, I'm the greeter and I have to wait right here.

I'll see you at our rookie's meeting tonight at eight in the front room. Oh, Abra, you're going to love Jackson and I think there are loads of guys who're going to love having you here. You're so appropriate!!" She gushed the praise as though it were a famous fact. It sounded so true. No one had ever known Abra suitable earlier than. People had talked about how smart she became and the way type she turned into, however by no means how she seemed. Her notion was that Laura is probably visually impaired. And definitely, nobody had ever called her honey. Most assuredly, she turned into the South now.

With hammering coronary heart and sweat-soaked fingers, Abra walked to room 234. She was full of the apprehension that each university newcomers sense upon assembly their new roommate, but more. She became packed with tension about entering the brand new world she so wanted to match into. The door changed into extensive open and a lady was standing on a mattress unpacking her suitcase. When she turned around, Abra noticed that the girl's face become included with freckles making her seem like a baby celebrity of a sitcom approximately the "common" American own family. Abra had by no means met everybody with so many freckles. Freckles have been no longer huge in Queens. As soon as she saw Abra, the woman's twinkling blue eyes exploded and he or she ran to Abra and hugged her tightly. "I'm thrilled to meet you. It's Abra with the lengthy a – right? What a unique name. Not like undeniable antique Beth." She right now started chattering. Beth turned into a congenital marathon talker. She by no means permit silences to slip right into a communication. She talked about the furnishings arrangement and showed how they could break up the whole thing in half.

"This mattress, cloth cabinet, and table are yours. Can you consider there's the best armchair? We ought to take turns sitting on every other's lap whilst we want to study." She waited for Abra to grin, and then continued, "I'm glad that we didn't have a hazard to get bedspreads and curtains earlier than we came. We need to get an experience of the room before we buy whatever. Later this week we'll go right down to Penny's. What do you believe you studied of yellow sunflowers like Van Gogh portray? I desire we can locate something like that." She didn't wait for a solution to hold. "We simplest have this one narrow window with that big tree blocking off out the solar. We need to liven up the room, but I think our glowing personalities will do masses to brighten up this area, don't you?" Abra didn't realize what Van Gogh's plants looked like. She became at a loss for what to say.

Fortunately, Miss Benjamin came in lugging a suitcase. She gave her common self-introduction. "Hi, I'm Edith Benjamin, Abra's cousin." Beth hugged her too as she apologized for her mother and father no longer being there to meet them. "My folks had to get back for my brother Jeff's baseball (generic term). He's the pitcher on his crew and he's in some kind of championship. I don't maintain track of all that jock stuff." Miss Benjamin presented, "I'm staying at the Bates Motel this night. Well, it's now not the Bates Motel, however, it positive does look a bit spooky. Anyhow, I'd like to have you be a part of Abra and me for an ultimate supper."

Beth replied, "I'd be elated. I hate the thought of being by myself on my first night time at university." Beth continually used the superlative. That turned into her method to life: revel in, find the high-quality anyplace it may lurk, and love to the maximum. Miss Benjamin left to test into the resort and said that she could pick out them up at 6:00 for dinner at a local steak residence. Abra, the ever-compulsive regulation abider, stated, "We ought to be back through eight. We can't be past due for our first meeting." Miss Benjamin gave her an understanding appearance and stated with mock annoyance, "Would I make you past due for your first meeting?" Abra nervously checked out her understanding that the time became getting close to, the time of her emancipation.

She unpacked as she and Beth chatted approximately the classes that they have been taking. As Abra talked, she felt a developing sense of happiness rise in her chest. She never felt happiness before, no longer even if she gave a speech representing the importance of character at the National Honor Society meeting or her thanks speech while she received two scholarships at the senior awards dinner. She felt this change in her body. She felt lighter. She felt like giggling. But unexpectedly she commenced to cry, to sob in uncontrollable spasms. Tears flooded her cheeks. Snot ran out of her nostril. She changed into leaking fluids from all elements of her face.

Beth at once hugged her. "Abra, don't cry. I understand the way you must experience it. You're unhappy and lonely being up to now from New York. You're probably questioning why on earth I picked this God-forsaken little college in the center of nowhere USA."

How incorrect Beth become! She changed into crying because she became being freed from incarceration, but she couldn't tell Beth. She couldn't tell all of us. Her tears had been washing away her past and he or she was feeling natural exhilaration and eagerness at starting her new existence.

They left their unpacking for later, and washed up, after which went all the way down to rock at the porch rockers and watch for Miss Benjamin to pick them up. Abra had never sat on a porch before. She knew that she could spend many hours rocking on this porch and searching out at the serene quad. The motion of the chair made Abra sense like a baby being rocked. How suitable for being born with brand new identification.

When Miss Benjamin picked them up, she took photos of the women in the rockers and several just Abra smiling. Then Beth took photographs of Miss Benjamin and Abra. How Abra valuable the one's pics, specifically those showing them hugging. She would examine them hundreds of times over the years. They documented this historic day in Abra's existence.

At dinner, they'd massive steaks. Miss Benjamin joked that this would be the final time that the women could have actual food and that they have to get prepared for institutional food now that they have been being institutionalized. All three girls laughed deeply as the seeds of friendship took root. Beth was so accepting of Abra. She didn't ask personal questions. She waited for Abra to volunteer information. Beth chatted non-forestall approximately England. "I spent the summertime with a family in north London. I become the nanny for their two youngsters. I become the American Mary Poppins. They had masses of dough and we traveled loads. We went to the Lake District and Scotland. I have a thousand billion images that I'll bore you with later. It turned into an existence-changing enjoyment. I wish you can go to England someday too." And while Abra went to England three years later, she, too, had an existence-changing experience.

Miss Benjamin mentioned her love of English ladies thriller writers. "Beth, you're now not the handiest Anglophile. I'm passionate about English girls' mystery writers. Have you heard of Dorothy Tey or Ruth Rendell? Of path, you haven't. Why would you? I'm making plans to go to England subsequent summer and journey to a number of the places these women have written about. I want you to give me the names of places you believe you studied I need to go to. Not many people get to spend two months residing and touring in England." Beth steered the conversation to a question about the relationship between Miss Benjamin and Abra. "How are you two associated?" Miss Benjamin explained, "Well we're distant cousins, but I was also Abra's newcomer English teacher. Abra's dad and mom are lifeless. Abra lived along with her grandparents and they couldn't drive her down so I volunteered." Abra had skilled Miss Benjamin to lie expertly. She was her co-conspirator. She turned into so accurate at this role that she would probably have handed a lie detector take a look. She had never objected to this position even though it need to have stricken her to lie when she was essentially an honest man or woman. Miss Benjamin knew that she should best be Abra's parent surrogate on Abra's terms.

Abra stated, "Even though Miss Benjamin's my cousin, I can't call her using her first call due to the fact she became my instructor. It sounds nutsy, but I just can't say, Edith. I generally call her Miss B." Beth said, "Then I'll call you Miss B too if that's ok with you." The three smiled as if agreeing no longer to go near to the actual trouble, Abra's own family. That became an issue to stay entombed for sixteen years. Like all and sundry who met Abra, Beth requested approximately the foundation of her call. "Abra, I've in no way heard that call earlier than. Where'd it come from?" Abra replied with her pat answer. "It's the lady form of Abraham. My parents had biblical names, Jacob and Miriam, and they wanted their first child to be named Abraham. Unfortunately, my gender made that name impossible so they took the first four letters and that's how I became Abra. I concept I was the simplest Abra in the world. At least, the only one which I knew of until Miss B brought me to Abra in John Steinbeck's East of Eden." When they arrived again at Lee Hall, Beth sensed that Abra desired to be by herself with Miss Benjamin for their desirable-byes so she hugged Miss Benjamin and told her that she turned into sure that she would see her once more. She became proper. She could see her oftentimes over the following sixteen years.

Miss Benjamin said that she turned into going to meet with Emily Weaver the subsequent morning, and then return home. "I'm having breakfast with Dr. Weaver. We may go to England together next summer season. Abra, I'm additionally going to ask her to be available for you if you need any help. I recognize you don't want me to try this, however, you by no means understand whilst you'll want a person regionally. I know which you're concerned that I'll tell her about your own family. I received."

There were oftentimes over the subsequent four years that Abra known as on Emily Weaver for help. Dr. Weaver became greater than a teacher. She, too, became a pillar of guide for Abra. Although she in no way knew the information about Abra's preceding existence, she had suspicions that Abra's simple description of her mother and father being useless concealed secrets and techniques.

Abra looked at Miss Benjamin and stated phrases that she by no means concept she could say to any man or woman, "I love you. You're my savior. Without you, I wouldn't have a lifestyle. I'll never be able to thank sufficient for what you've performed for me." Abra by no means shared feelings. That was no longer part of the lifestyle she had lived. When she instructed her dad and mom and grandparents that she changed to going away to college, they stated, "We want you. You can't pass." They didn't say we love you. Miss Benjamin couldn't communicate. Her glasses fogged up due to the endless glide of tears. Her jowls shook uncontrollably. Tall, thin Abra hugged short, plump Miss Benjamin. Miss Benjamin attempted to talk, but all that came out become "You're my daughter."

Abra stated, "Oh I so want you to have been my mother these last eighteen years."

CHAPTER THREE

Abra's four years at Jackson College had been a time of everyday exchange as she molded herself into the man or woman she dreamed of becoming. Her college life was a hemisphere away from her pre-college life. She in no way dreamed that it'd be so clean to head from hell to heaven in a seven-hour force. Abra was given up each morning taking into consideration simply one thing – herself. She didn't think of what she needed to do for her mother and father or Rachel or Noah. She was in the middle of the universe. And that is the way she desired her life to be all the time. Maybe it become egocentric, however, she felt that she had paid her dues of selflessness for the ultimate eighteen years.

During her freshman twelve months, she questioned approximately her family day by day. Were they eating nicely? Were they getting their drug treatments? Were Rachel and Noah doing okay at faculty? By her sophomore twelve months, she notion of them sporadically and by way of her junior twelve months, they have been nearly absolutely absent from her everyday awareness. She became surprised at how clean it have been to erase them from her existence. She felt like she have been born at age 18 whilst she entered Jackson College. She harbored no guilt approximately banishing her circle of relatives from her mental lifestyle as she had banished them from her physical lifestyle. This become what she needed to do to live on. She visualized the Ginzberg family as passengers on a sinking ship with one existence preserver. Abra slipped into it as she pried off the desperate grasping arms of Noah, Rachel, Jacob, and Miriam. At the cease of her reverie, she calmly watched her own family disappear into the icy water.

Abra popped off the bed each morning, alert and geared up to savor whatever the day might carry. The ladies in the dorm made fun of her suggesting that her invariably satisfied mood was attributable to chemical help. She insisted she turned into an herbal excessive and true-naturedly provided to take a drug test or have her room searched. Fortunately, Beth became like that too so that they have become known as the bubbly twins.

Some of those who knew Abra wondered why she didn't show any sadness approximately the dying of her circle of relatives, but they typically concluded that she changed into masking up her real feelings. A few even broached the problem with Beth. Sheila, a female who lived inside the next dorm room, once asked Beth: "Does Abra ever speak about her circle of relatives?" Beth answered plenty in the manner Abra could have if she were asked the question. "No. She doesn't want to share her emotions. She's coped together with her losses within the beyond and she's reached a level of popularity. She's shifting on with her lifestyles." Sheila pursued the difficulty. "It simply appears that on occasion she might show some sadness or negativity. She's just no longer normal. She's too fine. She's too glad, especially while you remember that her dad and mom are dead and she or he has no real family besides that fat woman."

"Abra's the maximum everyday individual I know. But she's additionally the most non-public. She doesn't need human beings to recognize her beyond and I recognize that. You should too." That positioned a cease to any conversations approximately Abra with Beth. But most people were still puzzled, handiest they didn't verbalize their questions to Abra or Beth. Sometimes in overdue night gossip fests, they conjured up tales about Abra's mother and father being murdered by a mad killer and Abra being the only survivor, or Abra's dad and mom being killed in an automobile accident, or Abra's father killing her mom after which committing suicide. A few went up to now as to fantasize that Abra killed her mother and father and did not should go to jail because she became going to Jackson and it became a penal institution. What Abra loved maximum about university changed into learning. She became the uncommon scholar who examine all the assignments as well as supplementary readings. Whenever feasible, she studied, in particular at some stage in the past due night hours when there has been generally quiet inside the dorm take a look at the room. No sounds coming from out of doors, no sounds from girls speaking, and no sounds from ladies sleeping. There became never total quiet in Queens, mainly on warm summer nights when people kept their home windows open attempting to find a fab breeze. On Seventeenth Street, Abra heard the summer night sounds of the town: whizzing window air conditioners, loud night breathing of sleep panics, crying of colicky infants, grunts and moans of sexual coupling, and arguments over infidelity or cash.

She cherished overdue nighttime analyzing whilst she communed with her books. She closed her eyes and concentrated on absorbing understanding via osmosis. She thrived on words and thoughts. She cherished writing papers so she should use phrases that she couldn't use in her normal speaking vocabulary. She created metaphors like "jaundiced leaves" in a freshman essay on what she favored about Jackson's campus. She could by no means say jaundiced leaves whilst dining along with her buddies over mac and cheese. She could hyperlink thoughts, locate reasons, undertake consequences, and become aware of relationships like an Olympic intellectual gymnast. She felt her mind cells multiplying as she studied. She loved herself when she studied because mastering was what she did best. She wished she may want to go to college forever.

Some of the girls inside the dorm kidded her about being an examination device and obsessed with grades. And certainly, she becomes an observation gadget and enthusiastic about grades. Doing properly in college had been the exit ramp from the life she despised. Doing properly in college became her way of validating herself as a smart individual who may want to acquire anything she wanted. Being smart differentiated her from her own family. She became the mutant in a circle of relatives of retarded human beings.

Abra started as an English main which was an herbal for her because of the affection for literature instilled in her by way of Miss Benjamin and her herbal skills for writing. But through conversations with Beth approximately her training, she became interested in psychology. So she brought psych as a second primary to become a toddler psychologist. She concept this will be a good professional match for her due to the fact she should empathize with kids going thru painful childhoods. She knew this will entail many years of education but it would result in an activity that Abra might usually want, having no one to lean on for a financial guide. She figured that there would continually be kids with troubles so there might always be a need for child psychologists.

During the summer after her junior year, Abra gained an opportunity to study in England for two weeks. She became to take a look at the London places featured in books by using predominant English writers. Abra didn't know that the money for the supply changed into donated by using Miss Benjamin who hooked up the supply with the information that Abra was the primary recipient. She is in no way suspected that the opportunity became funded through a specific donor, let alone Miss Benjamin. Thanks to her dad and mom's generosity, Beth followed Abra. After their weeks in London, they spent another week traveling via England. The existence-changing experience that Beth had defined that the first day they met three years in the past became a reality for Abra. In her four weeks in England, Abra had more memorable studies than she had in her preceding twenty-one years.

Getting her passport became a milestone in Abra's life. Now she had a worldwide identity. She may want to travel to the ends of the earth…journey in a jeep on a safari in Africa, scale the limitless steps of the Great Wall of China, or stand at the foot of Ayres Rock in Australia at sunset. Her passport image confirmed her joyous anticipation of the places she may want to move to. Her smile became so complete, that it monopolized the maximum of her face. Who could have an idea that she could pass from Seventeenth Street in Queens to the world? She would see places that the Ginzbergs in no way heard of, and even though they had, they wouldn't need to tour because there could be no bagels and TV soaps.

She had another first with this experience - her first aircraft flight. She and Beth flew out of Dulles Airport in Washington on a British Air 747. Beth's parents drove them to the airport and as they approached, Abra gasped at the splendor of Dulles. Its sloping roofs and its superbly contoured control tower had been works of art. Beth informed Abra, "Shut your mouth before you seize a fly. What are you going to do while you see Trafalgar Square – swallow a pigeon?"

Abra sat after the window with her nose glued to the glass. She delighted in the smallest things: the suitcases being loaded, the plane is fueled. As the aircraft started, her heart pounded, no longer with fear, but with anticipation. She cherished the feel of taking off. The noise of the engines and the gathering velocity filled her with elation. She sensed the warfare among her body being pulled up with the aid of the plane even as being pulled down using gravity. Flying changed into a manner of actually escaping, no longer simply metaphorically, but clearly. Beth despised flying. She effortlessly was given movement sickness so she had taken remedy to assist her with the U.S. and downs and shaking, rattling, and rolling. Beth slept a good deal of the manner and refused meals. Abra saved waking her up to quote from the guidebook on England which she had already read three instances. "Beth, wake up. Let's make certain that we rent a ship on the Avon when we go to Stratford. Let's also visit the Swan's Nest. It's over three hundred years antique. Hey, let's go to Marlowe's Restaurant. It's even older." Beth moaned and uncharacteristically advised Abra to fuck off as she burrowed into her pillow and blanket.

The flight was smooth as became the touchdown, even though now not to Beth. Abra appeared out the window and was given her first glimpse of London. Everything was gray, the sky changed into gray, the homes were gray, and even the streets had been grey. How ought something so drab be lovely? The first factor that struck her as she disembarked at Heathrow became the accents. These people without a doubt knew how to speak English. They didn't devour the language like New Yorkers. She felt so critical when the immigration agent requested what she turned into going to do in England. She crowed, "I'm going to tour your stunning U. S. A. And experience every second of it." Conveying whole boredom through his body language, he stamped her passport without searching up. She didn't allow his disinterest to dampen her enthusiasm. Nothing and no one turned into going to forestall her from having the excellent time of her existence.

The girls were given their luggage and took the tube from Heathrow to important London. Abra knew the New York subways nicely, but the tube changed into specific. It wasn't the cars or the people, it became simply the feeling of being foreign. During their stay in London, they took the subway regularly and always chanted "Mind the space" alongside the recorded message as they jumped over the gap between the platform and the education. Over the years, "mind the space" emerge as a sign between them to rekindle recollections in their ride.

They were given guidelines for on foot to their lodge on Bloomsbury Square. The Virginia Woolf Hotel. They have been staying at an inn in the community in which Virginia Woolf had lived. How perfect for an English important!

Perhaps they might see actual writers sitting within the square. How might they understand who turned into a creator? They in all likelihood could appear intellectual and wear berets and scarves jauntily wrapped around their necks. But, during their weeks in London, they didn't see anybody like that inside the park or for that rely everywhere on the metropolis. The park became packed with old people feeding the birds, college students studying textbooks, homeless people in fetal positions napping on benches, and nannies wheeling toddlers in prams. No overt intellectuals.

Beth and Abra shared a tiny room on the pinnacle floor with a window overlooking the rectangular. Abra spent each free minute searching out the window whilst she wasn't sound asleep or writing in her magazine. They shared a toilet with the alternative motel guests on the top ground. They were used to sharing a lavatory with girls at Jackson, however now they were sharing with guys. How continental! Because of the secure lock on the door, they by no means saw guys in any compromising positions. They have been disillusioned that they didn't see any nude or semi-nude guys taking walks back and forth to the restroom.

Every morning they were served an English breakfast of eggs, tomatoes, and kippers. On the first day, Abra tried everything, but she couldn't do it again. Abra hated fish, and kippers were the remaining fish. Kippur had been worse than gefilte fish. Warm tomatoes also didn't do something for her flavor buds. And slippery eggs fried in an unknown substance were too difficult for Abra to swallow, literally. She overlooked her Cheerios and bloodless milk.

Abra hadn't planned on snoozing for the two weeks they were in London, however as quickly as she have become horizontal she fell asleep. When she woke up six hours later, she became freezing. Although it became July, it became fifty degrees in London. Not most effective changed into it bloodless, it changed into damp. The type of dampness that makes your bones and inner organs shiver. They had introduced rain jackets expecting London's common wet weather, but no longer sweaters as it were ninety stages at home. So their first purchases were heavy sweaters to hold heat. It became so bloodless for a few nights that they slept with their sweaters over their pajamas. Beth's sweater became mainly ratty because it had remnants of pigeon poop from Trafalgar Square that refused to be washed out. After four weeks in England carrying their sweaters, they deposited them in a garbage bin at Heathrow earlier than boarding their aircraft for domestic. They had a rite as they buried their filthy sweaters with Beth officiating: "We officially positioned to rest our bulwark towards the brutal bloodless of the British Isles. It stored these two colonists from developing icicles on their tits."

Abra had an in-depth list of places she needed to visit for her provide, however she also desired to look at the "huge" traveler spots so they went to Buckingham Palace, Parliament, the Tower of London, and the British Museum. Abra imagined herself as a character everyplace they visited. At Buckingham, she was Princess Di. She couldn't consider herself as stiff Queen Elizabeth, specifically because she didn't have a purse; simplest a backpack that become difficult to hold over her wrist. At the Tower of London, she was Anne Boleyn getting her head lopped off. At the British Museum, she turned into a shapely version of an Elgin marble Greek goddess with frame elements shed over lots of years.

They went to plays nearly every night seeing Le Miss, Miss Saigon, and The Merchant of Venice. They treated themselves to high tea on the Waldorf, the final in British classiness. At domestic, Abra most effectively drank tea while she had a chilly, but in England she daintily sipped tea. At home, it was Lipton's teabags. In London, it becomes Fortnum and Mason's, Earl Grey. And of course, scones with clotted cream. Years later whilst she started frequenting Starbucks wherein scones were offered, she by no means offered any. She observed that she honestly didn't just like the flavor of scones, or perhaps the flavor of American scones. And she clearly wouldn't clot her arteries with correctly named clotted cream.

Both were in contact with the English own family with whom she had lived three years in advance. Hugh and Judith Fox and their two children, Frederick now ten, and Vanessa eight, lived in Hampstead Garden Suburb, a community of antique townhouses in North London that Old Forest Hills in Queens become modeled after. What an irony for Abra, she changed into journeying to a neighborhood in London that looked like a neighborhood near where she had lived for eighteen years. The Fox's domestic seemed like something out of a 1950 British black-and-white movie. They had a gas hearth that they used for warmth, now not decoration, lamps with fringe at the sun shades, and a kitchen sink with a separate faucet for hot and bloodless water. Abra notion the area become quaint, but no longer someplace should she live lengthy-term. She was too American; she cherished her conveniences.

They spent a Sunday with the Foxes taking walks through a park, reminiscing approximately Beth's in advance live. The climate had at last warmed up and the sun made an uncharacteristic look so they had tea at an outdoor café. Abra treasured the enjoyment of truly learning Brits and being more than a traveler who simply considered Brits as specimens. They ended the day with a fish and chips meal at a nearby restaurant. Abra insisted that she cherished the fried cod and French fries despite the grease that lined her hands and face.

Before leaving the states, the ladies had offered a British Rail skip which enabled them to freely travel thru England and Scotland. First, they went to Stratford on Avon and saw Macbeth at the Shakespeare Theatre. They respectfully visited Shakespeare's church and Ann Hathaway's residence and, of direction, the Swan's Nest and the Marlowe's. In the house in which Shakespeare turned into born, they touched the walls inside the wish that Shakespeare had also touched them. Despite the masses of years of paint and washing, they had been positive that their skin may want to experience Shakespeare's pores and skin. Abra remembered her vow to lease a ship so they were given a rowboat and rowed on the Avon as they sang "Row, row your boat." Not precisely a British ditty, but the only boating song they knew.

They traveled thru the Lake District traveling to villages on scenic lakes. On a warm, cloudless day in Keswick, they hiked ten miles around Lake Derwen water. But one of their most memorable reports of the experience changed into telling ghost memories in a church cemetery at nighttime. They had been staying in a student hostel where they met four college kids from New Zealand. One night, one of the boys recommended going to the church graveyard in the direction of their hostel to the lake. It turned into clean, crisp nighttime with a complete moon, ideal for ghost searches. The kids examine the information at the gravestones earlier than selecting the ones that they might grace with their backsides. Abra picked the everlasting resting place for Abigail Bennett, a year antique infant who died in 1826 whilst Beth picked her mom Sarah who lived for eighty-six years, a completely long time in the 1800s. Sarah had outlived her daughter using eighty-four years, how sad each of these years ought to be for Sarah.

Each of the cemetery haunters took turns telling ghost testimonies. Abra told the story of the headless horseman. Beth chastised her for no longer taking into account something authentic, but she advised the Stephen King story of Carrie causing Abra to punch her arm and return an insult about her lack of creativity. Abra may want to have stayed inside the cemetery until daybreak, however, the organization was affected by frostbitten feet so they went lower back to the hostel at about 2:00. As Abra lay in bed that night time, she found out that she should never have imagined this night's experience when she was lower back on 17th Street. Unimaginable – the phrase shapes the enjoyment and the word suit her existence because she left Queens on August 22nd, 1990.

After Keswick, they went to Edinburgh where they visited castles and walked the hills. They strolled along Princess Street, first buying on one side after which sitting on the benches under the citadel on the opposite. On their first day on Princess Street, Abra saw a group of mentally retarded adults with their caregivers. They have been searching in the shop home windows at Jenner's Department Store and describing what they saw. "I would like that blue sweater," stated a female with Down's Syndrome talking with a thick Scotch brogue, at the same time as an elderly guy with a small, misshapen head, stated, "I would like that yellow tie for Christmas." They all smiled as they held hands with every other and the caregivers. They appeared so glad and "regular" for retarded humans. Abra became away due to the fact she didn't need the mind of her family intruding on her happiness. She didn't want to examine Scottish and American retardation.

Just as Abra worked on developing her thoughts, she worked on developing her social capabilities. She developed a knack for making human beings sense comfortable and crucial. This mixed with her warm and bubbly way made her famous and well appreciated. Although she had many friends, she and Beth were inseparable. Beth was her genuine love, now not a gay love due to the fact each girl had no preference for each other bodily. They cherished every different like sisters, but in a different way. You don't get to pick out your sister. They had picked every other. They have been sharing studies that were molding them into the ladies they could end up and because of this, they were intertwined like a latticed mountain climbing vine.

Over the four years of college, Beth two times broached the issue of Abra's family, and each time Abra close her out. One night time after they were discussing "deep thoughts," Beth requested, "Do you think a whole lot about your mother and father?" "I just can't speak approximately that. Please, permit's not move there. You recognize how painful that is for me to talk approximately." "I'm sorry. I recognize." But she didn't apprehend. She thought that high-quality friends need to share the whole lot, however, Abra believed that best buddies ought to proportion the entirety, except for an afflicted beyond.

Another time, the two girls have been mendacity under the stars at Beth's family's seashore residence whilst Beth stated "Do you suspect your mother and father are up there?" "I attempt now not to consider my dad and mom." Beth become tempted to ask why no longer, however, she knew that Abra had closed herself off. She turned into positive that in the future Abra would proportion her secrets and techniques, however perhaps no longer till they were old ladies in a nursing home.

Occasionally, Abra mentioned her grandparents, specifically when she acquired her monthly letter from them with two crisp ten-dollar payments enclosed. She would reply with thanks notes containing some comments about how college became going or the weather. Abra talked loads about Miss Benjamin. She has been Abra's own family during her high faculty years. Abra had eaten at Miss Benjamin's condominium in some of the instances and they had gone to the theatre and concert events together. During her four years at Jackson, Abra spent some of her school holidays at Miss Benjamin's when she didn't go to Beth's house or stay in Linz.

Although Abra never mentioned her circle of relatives, Beth regularly disclosed increasingly more approximately her own family. Abra looked at the King's circle of relatives as clones of the Brady Bunch. But Beth progressively shared family secrets and techniques displaying to Abra that even the most "normal" circle of relatives had skeletons in their closets. There had been the usual own family feuds between Beth's mom and her aunt and the alcoholism of a grandfather, but the King's important issue revolved around Beth's brother Jeff's homosexuality. Jeff, a year younger than Beth, turned into also at Jackson where he was captain of the baseball group and a tune megastar. He became a film-famous person precise looking and had the body of a gymnast. All the ladies on campus lusted after Jeff, and Jeff lusted after all the boys. In his freshman year, Jeff informed Beth that he become gay. Beth turned no longer surprised; she had continually suspected. It wasn't whatever he stated or did, perhaps it turned into gaydar. He hadn't instructed his dad and mom due to the fact they had been devout Christians who believed that homosexuality was sinful. His father who had been athletic all his life couldn't consider that a jock, like Jeff, might be homosexual. It could be a few years before Jeff would eventually tell his dad and mom. When he sooner or later did, his father became the demise of cancer. He instructed Jeff that he had always recognized in his heart, however, couldn't brazenly renowned that his son turned into a homosexual. The day earlier than he died, he told Jeff that he would like him for eternity and so would God.

As part of developing the lady she turned into becoming, Abra labored on developing a unique look. She became slowly realizing that she changed into placing, not lovable or pretty, however appealing, someone humans took a second to take a look at. With her dark complexion, small upturned nostrils, massive black eyes, and tall, trim figure, she became almost beautiful. She wore undeniably, but pricey, clothes, and tee shirts generally in preppy colorations with a polo participant on her chest. In Queens, she had shopped at stores wherein she may want to purchase garments for less than $10.00. There is no way to become cash for clothes or earrings. She became always ashamed of the garments she wore. Although she nevertheless didn't have an awful lot of money, now she shopped at the Gap and the Banana Republic wherein she sold at massive reductions at the give up of the season. Miss Benjamin knew her love of top clothes and gave her a generous gift certificate for the Gap for Hannukah and her birthday so she could dress in a manner proper to the person she desired to venture to the sector. She loved searching at herself inside the mirror, now not only for how she looked but for who she become becoming. Her new outer look complemented her new inner self.

During their school years, Abra changed into a work take a look at scholars inside the English branch and worked for Dr. Weaver. During the summertime, she helped the Jackson groundskeepers tend the flower beds. The cash that she made combined with her scholarships and loans made it feasible for her to get via. As in high faculty, she worked in the newspaper finally turning into an information editor. Now the occasions she wrote approximately within the paper were activities that she witnessed firsthand. Dances, lectures, sports activities. The stuff of college existence. In high school, she wrote about these occasions, however, experienced them vicariously. Now she mentioned them and lived them.

Everyone at Jackson turned into some recreation so Abra selected strolling. She was an extremely good walker on the streets of Queens so now she just went faster. A lot of kids ran to loosen up, however, Abra was never disturbed. She had no tension about her training or the future. She favored jogging because of the sensation of freedom. She ran all over campus which increased to the streets of the small town after which to the U. S. Roads. She became nevertheless amazed at seeing cows and chickens at the farms she handed. These were the real animals that she had to examine with Rachel. When she noticed them, she could make the sounds – moo, quack, and oink. She might consider Rachel whilst she did this and the way she might respond to seeing actual animals, no longer photographs. She might probably cry and balk with worry. Rachel turned frightened of everything new and one-of-a-kind, in contrast to her sister who treasured the whole lot as new and distinctive.

Another of Abra's achievements in university turned into studying to force. Lots of human beings in Queens did not have power. They took subways or buses and for special activities, cabs or private vehicles. Beth had her car in their junior twelve months and taught Abra to power in a single clean lesson. Abra pored over the drivers' manual, took the written take a look at and, of course, surpassed it with one hundred percent. When she exceeded the behind-the-wheel check, she became deliriously happy. She hugged the bored tester who reacted as if he were sexually attacked. Abra's picture on her motive force's license changed into like her passport photograph showing a broadly smiling woman geared up to see the world in a car driven via her.

Over their four years collectively, Abra and Beth deliberate how they could have all the reports vital to grow to be worldly women. Now they have been seniors and nonetheless virgins. They couldn't name themselves worldly girls while not having skilled sex. They both had dated however hadn't discovered all of us that they in reality liked or that they desired to don't forget as their first. They had been determined to lose their virginity before graduating. Like everything else in their lives, they made careful plans. They investigated going on the tablet or getting a diaphragm or using a condom or using all three. They were cautious approximately their lives and wanted to make sure that they were covered from being pregnant and disease. They were keen for intercourse, but cautious intercourse.

Fate looked kindly on Beth's quest for her first sexual experience. She met Tom Newland who could turn out to be the affection of her life in addition to her first and best intercourse accomplice. Tom had graduated from a university in Pennsylvania the year earlier and became now a graduate scholar at UVA where he became getting a master's degree and kingdom licensure to teach records. He became coaching a freshman history class at Jackson and operating as a waiter in a newly opened pizza parlor. Beth and Abra went to try out the pizza and they observed Tom. He changed into built like the wrestler he has been in high faculty and university. He regarded a piece like Beth because he, too, had thick darkish blond hair and masses of freckles. They may want to have passed for siblings, maybe that's why they had been at once interested in each other. As he served them their pizza and liquids, he flirted with Beth, and earlier than they left, Beth agreed to peer, Tom, the following night. After a movie, he took Beth lower back to his apartment and she or he had her first sexual enjoyment. In the beyond she had worried approximately whether to kiss a guy on the primary date and now she had sex on her first date. Within every week, Beth turned head over heels in love with Tom. She unreservedly extolled the virtues of intercourse, vividly describing every element from Tom disposing of her garments to her climaxes. Abra was surprised at her reaction. She became green with envy. She wanted a fairy story to revel in like Beth's. For the first time in her college life, she wanted something she couldn't get by way of planning.

Abra looked at every guy with a specific motive. Would he be proper as her first? A man in her psych of persona elegance was thrilling, however, she appreciated his thoughts, no longer his frame. He changed into a scarecrow and even though his penis is probably the proper length, the rest of him turned into too skeletal. Another guy she ran with had an incredible body, however, become as dumb as a dog. He didn't must make wise communication, but she desired her first to be someone with an IQ over one hundred. She was worried that she changed into being too picky and with the end of the school year speedy drawing near, she would omit these one major lifestyles enjoy. She didn't need to graduate as a twenty-two-year-old virgin.

Tom instructed the women about a guy in his grad application who Abra might like. He also knew of Beth and Abra's plan to lose their virginity earlier than commencement. Although Abra didn't like blind dates, she turned eager to meet this guy due to the fact he might be someone as exact as Tom. Rick Carbona from New Jersey grew to become out to be pretty not like Tom. He changed into operating on a doctorate in records at UVA and became teaching two records training at Jackson. Abra thought he was okay searching – darkish-haired, darkish-skinned, fine functions, and muscular construct. Two troubles – he turned into a brief, probably two or 3 inches shorter than she, and from what she ought to see of his fingers and chest where his blouse collar opened, he changed into covered with thick black frame hair. Even his arms had been bushy. She determined all that hairiness ape-like.

The four of them went to a beer joint to listen to a rock band. Abra didn't take note of the band. They could have been gambling Beethoven for all she knew. Abra became centered on Rick even when she wasn't speaking to him or looking at him. At the end of the evening, Rick requested Abra out for the following Saturday night time. All week, she and Beth pointed out whether he might be the one.

Abra became enthusiastic about what she could put on Saturday night and the way she would react to what he would possibly do. Should she cooperate if he took off her clothes? Should she provoke intercourse if he didn't? At Victoria's Secret, she bought an attractive crimson lace bra and matching bikini pants, very distinct from her normal white cotton undies. As she looked at her textbooks, she fantasized scenarios of passionate lovemaking on a luxurious mattress protected with satin sheets with Rick lightly eliminating her stunning new underclothes and commenting, "This bra and panties are fantastic, similar to you." In her fantasies, Rick turned hairless.

At final, Saturday night time arrived. Abra met Rick inside the lobby of her dorm. Her hands were dripping with sweat. She became glad he didn't contact her. He had a VW Beetle that regarded adored it became new in 1960.

He changed into well-mannered and opened the auto door for her. What a fantastic start. They went to Charlottesville where he lived because there has been a new restaurant he desired to strive for. He said he was a maven of Italian cooking and he desired to assess it. She knew that the real reason they have been going to Charlottesville was to be close to his condominium. Their dinner in the restaurant became fun. The meal was precise and Rick become a fantastic conversationalist with a biting humorousness. As they left the restaurant, he said, "Now to my vicinity for dessert." He leered at her and he or she knew what dessert he become planning. She felt as though she have been about to bungee bounce off a bridge. There was no turning back.

His rental was squalid, like that of maximum grad students. He lived in two rooms in a divided house with a couple of apartments. No sumptuous mattress with satin sheets – just an unmade unmarried mattress driven in opposition to a wall and dirty garments piled on the floor. As soon as they entered the apartment, he pulled Abra to the couch and stated, "Let's get down to business. Your first time and I'll make it first-rate for you. You'll usually consider it." "How did you know it's my first time?" "You introduced it to Tom and he advised me."

He kissed her deeply his tongue touching her tonsils. Then he pulled her purple polo up and massaged her breasts. Before she could stop him, he had her bra pulled up above her breasts. He hadn't even checked out her lacy new buy. He became shifting so speedy. It turned as if he had six fingers. She was sexually aroused and didn't want him to forestall, however, she didn't want this to move too fast. She wanted it to be leisurely and romantic and memorable.

Before she knew it, he had pulled down her khakis and her lacy bikinis. He spread her legs huge and pressured himself into her. With some deep lunges into her unexplored vagina, he got here. Abra looked down and saw that she had bled on his couch. "Geez, I'm sorry. Look what I did on your couch."

Laughing, he stated "This old piece of shit. It's been screwed on hundreds of instances and has the evidence permanently embedded within the cloth."

She positioned her clothes returned in order and went to the bathroom to clean herself with the use of tissues given that there has been no washcloth that she could see. It took half a container earlier than the blood was gone. There become simplest one grimy towel to dry herself. She cringed at the idea of what else was dried with this rag. She used extra tissues to dry herself.

When she was given again out, she saw that Rick was asleep on the mattress. She sat on the sofa, far from the bloody remains of her virginity. She became sweaty and disoriented. This became now not what she expected. This became a horrible enjoyment. She didn't know what to make of the feelings in her vagina. She felt a throbbing ache, however additionally a tingling that wouldn't forestall. She cried silently and dozed off. Sometime later, Rick becomes pulling her off the sofa. "Come directly to the mattress. It's snugger." He guided her to the mattress and stated, "Take off your garments." She obeyed hoping that this time could be higher. He got onto the mattress and right now got on the pinnacle of her. With minimum foreplay, he entered her and pumped up and down for what appeared like hours whilst he grunted. He never checked out her or talked to her. As he become doing this, she checked out him and thought she turned into coupling with an ape. Finally, he came. Then he asked, "Want to sleep over or cross back to Linz?"

Without hesitation, Abra replied, "Let's move lower back." She needed to break out from him. On the manner lower back he chatted about college and movies while Abra stared out into the darkness questioning what she had done. She didn't feel disgraced. She felt raging anger at herself for essentially advertising and marketing that she was geared up for sex with everybody inclined and in a position. Her first sexual come upon became not anything as she dreamed of. It became impersonal, grungy, and mechanical. When they were given to the dorm, he stated, "Can I see you subsequent Saturday? I assume we should be suitable together. It gets higher with exercise. You'll discover ways to like it." Abra told him to name her later within the week, knowing that she by no means wanted to peer him again. When she got to her room, Beth turned asleep, however, got up as quickly as she heard Abra input. "Tell me all approximately it. I can't wait to pay attention to what befell." "I need to take a protracted bath first. Just allow me to say that I did not have an evening with satin sheets."

After a protracted soak inside the bath with repeated washings of her vagina, accompanied using a shower in which she washed her hair twice, she placed on smooth white, cotton underpants and pajamas. She climbed into bed and stated, "He acted like an ape and I felt like an animal just screwing and being screwed. Beth, I'm hoping that one-day intercourse can be amazing, but it needs to be with someone I like and now not just for the sake of intercourse. That's not me. Maybe, I shouldn't have been so eager to have each experience earlier than graduating. But now I am a properly-knowledgeable girl who has traveled abroad and who has had sex, albeit no longer exact intercourse, however sex. I'll tell you the sordid info the following day." With that, Abra fell right into a deep sleep without romantic desires.

Her senior year delivered plans for grad faculty. She was ranked third inside the senior magnificence and had high GRE rankings so she had no problem getting money for Grad College. Originally, Beth and Abra were going to visit grad faculty together. Now Beth became tied to Tom who got an activity teaching high college history outdoor of Richmond. Beth decided to visit VCU in Richmond so she and Tom could stay together till they saved sufficient money to marry.

Abra determined to visit grad faculty at the University of South Carolina in Columbia. She has been provided a graduate assistantship that would pay her tuition plus living prices. She additionally favored the concept of USC as it changed farther from Queens to Virginia. When she went down to fulfill the school and her advisor, she also met Judy Hurley, every other new grad pupil, who requested to room with her. She knew that she would in no way find some other Beth, however, Judy seemed friendly and smooth going. The reality that she turned into black changed into going to offer Abra some studies in cultural diversity which she sorely wished for. Her enjoyment of numerous cultures became limited to New York Jews and Christian Virginians.

During her senior year, Abra legally changed her ultimate call from Ginzberg to Berg. This turned into her manner of formally becoming any other person. She changed her school data to Berg and all of her paperwork for grad school become within the name of Berg. She was given a brand new passport with the call Berg even though she wasn't planning on visiting abroad. When she got to South Carolina, she got a driver's license with the name Abra Berg. Now she turned into completely Abra Berg.

Graduation was a bittersweet day for Abra. She didn't want her existence at Jackson with Beth to quit, but at the same time, she was ready to transport directly to the subsequent phase of her existence. Miss Benjamin came for the weekend festivities. She attended the honors feast and the commencement rite as Abra's family.

After the commencement ceremony, Beth, Tom, Beth's own family, Abra, Dr. Weaver, and Miss Benjamin went for lunch at the same steak residence wherein they had eaten on August twenty-second four years earlier. Miss Benjamin took countless pictures of Abra in her cap and gown and Abra along with her hands round all and sundry else. Years later, Abra might study these photos and compare them to the photos of herself on her first day at Jackson. To her, they have been before- and after-images. The before-pix showed her hopeful anticipation at what awaited her at Jackson, and the after-pix showed her happiness for the person she had created. Others might observe the pictures and simplest see that Abra wore more make-up and greater stylish clothes, however, they wouldn't see the actual changes inner. The earlier than-pics confirmed a woman with four humans soaring over her shoulder seeking to grasp her. The after-snap shots showed not anything behind the girl. She changed into loose. She wanted to usually keep in mind the moment that capped the happiest four years of her lifestyle. She wanted to take into account the look of whole success on her face. She had executed everything she had dreamed of and even things she couldn't have imagined. Unimaginable to Abra Ginzberg of Queens.

Arm in arm, Abra and Beth walked along with the quad for the remaining time. They talked about how their lives could be for all time intertwined. Abra told Beth that she would like her for the rest of her existence and would even die for her. Beth laughed and knew that she would due to the fact she, too, could die for Abra. Beth stated "We were so fortunate to have such happiness. Nothing went wrong in our lives these closing four years, properly besides your first sexual enjoyment which changed into a fiasco. Now we have to assume matters to trade. As higher than all people, lifestyles isn't simplest good things. It's also an unpleasant and sad thing. We'll have illness or demise or things move incorrectly. But I hope we'll constantly be there for each other if anything takes place." And they were.

CHAPTER FOUR

Abra and Beth were in training all day at the conference on Friday. They attended classes during the day and the night and had supper with Abra's antique pals from her USC doctoral program. On Saturday, they endured with education classes however grew to become down gives to have dinner. They had made a reservation at Azalea's, one of Abra's preferred Charleston eating places. Over their first glass of wine, they chatted approximately the convention, after which Abra moved the communique to the real cause for his or her dinner.

"It's time, Beth. A final. It's time for me to inform you approximately my past. You knew the day would come after I would tell you my secrets. Well, that is the day. I am so sorry that I hid my life from you. I just couldn't inform you of all of the awful things in my existence. Something terrible befell this week. It's why I turned into past due getting right here." Once she started her confession, Abra determined that words gushed out on their personal. She felt like a Catholic sinner at confession.

"My parents aren't dead like I've constantly instructed you. I have a brother and a sister or just a brother now. My sister died this week. I noticed a piece of writing about her in the New York Post when I was at National anticipating my aircraft to come here so I modified my plans and went to New York to peer her funeral, however, I didn't visit the funeral. I went to get a glimpse at what passed off because I left in 'ninety when I went away to Jackson. I saw my parents and my brother. They didn't see me." She snickered as she stated, "I felt like a stalker."

They stopped to eat and chat with the waiter approximately how top the grouper was, but all that turned into only a diversion earlier than they may get lower back to Abra's revelations. "My dad and mom are alive. My dad's physically disabled. There's something incorrect with his again and he's bent over. He's been on disability for that all time. He's additionally what we experts might don't forget a slow learner, or maybe mildly intellectual retarded. He can handle everyday intellectual activities, however now not a whole lot greater. He didn't graduate from high college. He worked as a loader placing newspapers on trucks until he again went out. He changed into surprisingly normal whilst he married my mother." She drew out each syllable in the phrase "distinctly."

As she spoke, she recalled a photo of Jacob lying on the sofa. Her recollections have been frequently based totally on snapshots she hadn't visible for the reason that she left home, but were completely etched in her thoughts. She didn't know why her grandmother wanted to record the squalor of the Ginzberg hellhole and its unsmiling occupants. The few pics she took outdoor the residence were of Abra being honored at college ceremonies. There had been no pix of vacations due to the fact there were no holidays. There were no photos of journeys to the zoo because there were no trips to the zoo. The circle of relatives stayed internal and watched TV, besides for Abra who stayed inner and studied.

Jacob sincerely becomes a couch potato. As she recalled

images of him over time, she noticed how he had grown heavier and greater bowed. She usually notion of him on that identical inexperienced tweed couch. It was given so filthily over the years. No one ever thought of having a brand new one or re-upholstering it. When it became too badly worn, they included it with an itchy wool afghan her grandmother had knitted.

Abra remembered that her father regularly had this clean expression on his face like he was bored. But Abra didn't assume he changed into bored, she notion he didn't have any mental pastime going on. When he wasn't watching TV, which turned rare, he just stared into the area. As she thought of her father, she realized that she had no idea who Jacob Ginzberg turned into. With all her mental training, she didn't recognize him, possibly because she had in no way wanted to. She didn't want to apprehend that her father, the source of half of her genes, turned into mildly mentally retarded.

"Jacob's passion was my mom Miriam. He doted on her as she turned into a toddler. He surely in no way doted on any of his children. He overlooked us the maximum of the time. I assume he turned satisfied that Miriam married him and had intercourse with him, nicely as a minimum of three times. Although he had a problem taking walks, he changed into always serving her meals and assisting her with the little cleaning they did. I did most of the cleaning and trust me that wasn't a good deal. The region was a pigsty. Maybe that's why I'm so compulsively easy now. You continually made a laugh of me for cleansing our room all the time. You said college students aren't purported to smooth their rooms. That turned into actual if they came from smooth houses. That dorm room was my first smooth environment.

Jacob always talked to Miriam approximately their TV packages. Did she just like the new characters on the soaps they watched all day? Did she like what befell at the exceptional sit-down-coms they watched all night time? Did she like the visitors on Geraldo or Oprah? The TV changed into constantly on, no longer as heritage, but as mental sustenance. They watched the whole thing, even quiz shows wherein they didn't know the answers or even apprehend the questions. They observed all the soaps and knew everybody's lifestyle issues on General Hospital and All My Children. They watched Oprah even if she had politicians or authors discussing concepts they couldn't begin to recognize. Other than me, no person read an e-book or a newspaper. No one mentioned global activities. No one asked me what I studied in school. For them, the arena best existed on TV.

Now my mom didn't spend her days and nights sitting on the couch. She sat on a chair at the kitchen table adjacent to the residing room. That become so she should use the ashtray at the desk as she chain-smoked one cigarette after every other whilst preserving her eyes on the TV. Thanks to her that house becomes like a smoke-crammed bar, enveloping everyone and the whole lot in lung-clogging smoke. I get quick of breath simply thinking about the air pollution in that small rental. Even the EPA might claim condo 2A had toxic surroundings.

Miriam becomes genuinely retarded. I'd say her IQ became sixty to seventy. Her oral language becomes tough to apprehend even whilst you had been around her for a long time. She had masses of articulation substitutions and developmentally her language become like a seven or eight-year antique. She also had the end-toe, ahead leaning gait that we see with some kinds of neurological impairment. Her brother had equal characteristics so I understand that her disability was genetic. He died young. I don't surely bear in mind plenty about him, just the stroll. I can't consider his call. Isn't that terrible? He turned into my uncle and I won't forget his name and I don't care.

I would pass for days without speaking to Miriam or maybe searching for her. When we talked, it was about what I needed to get at the shop or what I had to do for the children. We never pointed out me and my life. Well, I didn't have tons of life. I just had school which I gobbled."

She had a problem picturing her mom despite the snapshots her grandmother had taken. She attempted to stay away from her mom due to the cigarette smoke and the disdain she felt toward her. No, she felt blinding hatred closer to her. She wasn't sure how her parents felt about her. Her idea was that perhaps her father appreciated her, but she knew that her mother hated her, probably because she changed into intimidated by using Abra's intelligence. Abra becomes an alien who became so exceptional from every person in their own family. She knew that all of them wanted her. They needed Abra like drowning people need a lifestyles raft. You don't love an existence raft.

What an opposite state of affairs. Most families are made of ordinary humans with one disabled man or woman. Not Abra's. Her own family becomes made up of disabled people with one normal character. She turned into the oddity.

"Everyday life inside the Ginzberg residence changed into filled with consuming and looking TV. When my dad and mom interacted with Rachel and Noah, they screamed.

They never talked in a regular tone of voice. They in no way said kind phrases to them. They never smiled at them. When they spoke to me they used an everyday tone of voice, however, I never was given kind phrases or smiles, now not even when I introduced domestic perfect file cards.

I recognize you're wondering how they would get married. I'm sure their parents arranged it. They wanted them to have companionship in existence like everyone else. They knew that they wouldn't be assembling everyone at college or a bar or work. They each had menial jobs after they married. My mother's mother and father had been fairly well off and they made a massive wedding ceremony. I used to take a look at their wedding album all of the time. I couldn't believe these satisfied humans have been my dad and mom. My mom looked nearly quiet in her frilly, puffy wedding dress and her lacy veil. It turned into a gaudy wedding ceremony dress that you'd see at a Polish or Mexican wedding ceremony. My dad appeared sort of good-looking in his white tux, with tails no less. I think every person appears desirable in wedding ceremony photos."

She visualized the photos from the album. Were the ones virtually her dad and mom? They have been dancing and reducing the multi-tiered cake. There turned into a fantastic image of Jacob together with his foot raised high approximately to destroy the wine glass, the culmination of a Jewish marriage ceremony. Then there was the image that she checked out most customarily - the romantic kiss on the give up of the ceremony. Tall Jacob held quick Miriam in his hands, dipping her returned and giving her a juicy kiss. It changed into like a kiss from a vintage time movie. She couldn't don't forget seeing them kiss apart in that picture. The best time she recalled seeing them touch become after they posed for snapshots and Jacob put his arm around Miriam.

"They had me first. I developed early in all areas. My grandmother Joyce, my dad's mom, kept a baby album with all my milestones. She changed into so proud that Jacob and Miriam produced an ordinary baby. Not simplest a normal infant, but a smart baby. She mentioned how I started to mention complete sentences after I was just over a year old, how I ought to matter to twenty at age two. I started to examine the first actual day of school. I probably would have examined earlier than the faculty however there have been no books at domestic for me to read. I constantly were given A's and turned into on the honor roll. I wonder how properly I did at faculty without any stimulation at home. We constantly speak about how children want to have an educationally supportive home to do well in the faculty. I didn't have an educationally supportive domestic. No books, no journeys to museums, no stimulating conversation, no encouragement to do my first-rate academically. Just people looking at the TV all the time. How the hell did I achieve this properly in faculty? How did I grow to be one of the smartest children in my class? I truly can't explain it.

No one from my home ever went to instructor meetings so none of my teachers ever noticed my mother and father. When Rachel and Noah started the unique Educational lessons, social people and special Education instructors made home visits. They saw the hellhole in which we lived. I'm positive they shared what they saw at the Ginzbergs with the other instructors at college, and I'm positive I became the topic of many discussions in trainer lounges through the years.

I'm a living argument for the nature aspect within the ever-popular nature-nurture trouble. Somehow I was given smart genes that made it feasible for me to thrive regardless of my impoverished surroundings. I ought to be a mutation due to the fact four of the five Ginzbergs were given dirty genes. That's how I think about my own family. I got the starched, glowing smooth jeans and they got the grimy wash. Go figure."

She visualized a picture of herself while she became a senior in high college that induced a vibrant recollection. She became standing after Mr. Boyers, the principal, who became offering her a plaque for being editor-in-leader of the college newspaper. She wore a red sweater set and a protracted gray skirt, her uniform for all of the senior events where she become honored. Her outward expression was constantly the same, a wide smile. But if you peered into her eyes you would see a confusion of emotions, broadly speaking soreness and a feeling of no longer belonging and a want to getaway.

She twirled her wine glass and said, "When I was a senior, I turned in the awards application and Mr. Boyers, the predominant, was creating a speech approximately me. How I changed into within the pinnacle five percent of the magnificence, had two scholarships, and was one of the quality editors-in-chief that the school newspaper ever had. Of direction, my mother and father weren't there. I wouldn't allow them to come even though they desired to. I knew that they would by no means come to something at faculty. That became the vicinity in which they failed. That changed into the vicinity that was alien to them. I didn't need them there. I didn't want everyone to look at them. God, it would be so humiliating and shameful if anybody saw them. My grandmother, Joyce, and my grandfather, Hal, have been sitting in the front row. They were beaming with delight. My grandfather became fumbling with the digital camera even as my grandmother noisily sobbed away.

Although my face became plastered with a smile, I felt shame. Shame for in which I came from and who I was. You're likely questioning that I should have felt delighted in overcoming my home life and reaching such fulfillment, however, I didn't experience a pleasure. I felt shame that I became produced by way of defectives. Mr. Boyers become taking place and on about how I have to experience terrific delight in my accomplishments. The unstated message become that I had triumphed over large obstacles. Everyone at college knew something approximately my home state of affairs, but no person ever mentioned it to me. Here he becomes now strongly intimates that I should experience pleasure in what I had attained considering my horrible home lifestyle. I wanted he could shut up and just let me be like all people else. After the presentation, he spoke with me and my grandparents and stated that I turned into an angel for what I did for my own family. He pretty much called me a martyr. I didn't have a preference. I couldn't run far from home then. I had to attend to them, however, that didn't make me an angel or a martyr, it made me a slave."

Beth interceded, "No, you're incorrect. You should have run away or you may have rebelled. Many children could have. You may want to have put your needs first, but you didn't. You have been being the coolest lady, that you've usually been Abra. I can't emphasize that enough. You've continually achieved the proper factor. You've usually been involved in ethical problems. For eighteen years you had been faced with Sophie's choice, which baby to shop for. For eighteen years, you picked Rachel and Noah and after that you picked yourself. There changed into no proper desire. But that becomes the right preference primarily based on your survival.

You are an emotionally robust man or woman, and that became what got you via those eighteen years. Other children with much less stability and internal electricity might have grown to become outward with the aid of appearing out with tablets or intercourse or grew to become inward by way of becoming depressed or self-unfavorable. What is so uncommon approximately you is that you were born with high intelligence AND a robust inner center. Your intellectual fitness is incredible. You don't smoke or drink, properly apart from an occasional Pinot Grigio. I'm positive you in no way took pot or tablets, as a minimum no longer on your four years at Jackson."

Abra commented, "I should be the best twelve months old Ph.D. Who in no way smoked pot? I did get some second-hand pot smoke even though. Remember Drew that man from Grad College who showed me correct sex? Well, he usually smoked pot once we had intercourse. I think I ingested enough from him. Does that rely on?" "No, it must be first-hand. And you've by no means taken psychotropic drugs. No anti-depressant, no anti-anxiety. Even with all of your issues about human beings locating out approximately your past and you still didn't need pills. Have you ever taken anything apart from aspirin?"

"Tylenol." "I think you gift two factors of the character-nurture problem, intelligence, and mental health. Genetically, you're proficient in both. Someone wishes to put in writing a piece of writing approximately you, but manifestly maintaining you nameless."

Abra requested the waiter for espresso. Her confession was draining her and he or she needed a little stimulation. "I need to reflect inconsideration on what you're pronouncing. You continually see different factors of things I never considered earlier.

Let me end my confession. I need to preserve talking or I'll clam up again. Let me tell you about Rachel and Noah, my secret siblings. I don't suppose there have been any infant albums for them. I don't consider seeing any. It has to have been obvious early on that they had been developmentally not on time. I suppose each person realized that Rachel and Noah have been clones of Miriam, most effective cognitively and more excessive. I sincerely don't recognize why they had Noah whilst it was obvious that Rachel become retarded like my mom. Someone ought to have had the best experience tying her tubes after Rachel turned born. Since they didn't have any extra children after Noah, I count on whether she did have her tubes tied or perhaps they didn't have sex anymore. Who is aware of it? Everyone continually says that they couldn't believe their parents having sex. Well, no person of their proper mind ought to believe Jacob and Miriam having sex. I recognize that humans of all cognitive tiers have sex drives, but I actually by no means noticed any evidence of that during my dad and mom. There become no physical affection between my parents and the kids. But my grandparents have been affectionate, but generally with me. After they retired, they got here over every day, besides when they went to the race tune, and once they came in the front door, they might say, 'Where're our kisses Abra?' And then they could cover me with juicy kisses. When they weren't looking, I'd wipe the saliva off my face.

They didn't try this with Rachel and Noah. Maybe because Rachel and Noah didn't ask for human contact from them, handiest from me. They had been usually climbing on my lap and putting their fingers around me. Sort of like octopus palms around my neck. I allow them to do it. Strange, they kissed me most of the time, and once in a while, they kissed my grandparents. They didn't kiss my dad or mum."

In the few images of Rachel and Noah as toddlers that Abra should remember, they have been lovely. With what she knew about toddler improvement now, she may want to recall the pictures of them with terrible head control well beyond the time when it became normal. She could bear in mind photos of them sitting and no longer on foot once they had full heads of hair and need to be two or three. She most vividly recalled their faculty snapshots. They constantly had these goofy smiles showing off their crooked teeth. No braces for these children even though the circle of relatives ought to have afforded it. They had been retarded and nobody tons cared approximately how they were regarded.

"My grandparents – my dad's parents - helped cope with each person. They lived within the condo construction next door and once they retired, they were always at the house. As I was given older, I took on greater responsibility. Or definitely, they made me take on greater responsibility. You can't imagine what I needed to do as a younger child. I need to be six or seven after I was converting Rachel and Noah's diapers and feeding them. They usually had behavior problems so I turned into constantly looking to make them sit down and consume or forestall throwing things or stop screaming or forestall biting. I evolved accurate conduct control abilities at an early age. Maybe that's why I'm so properly at running with E.D. children. As they grew older, their conduct troubles were given worse, particularly among faculty. There had been always social people and psychologists and teachers coming to the house and telling us the kind of behavioral program we had to set up at home so it might be steady with what turned into being accomplished at faculty. I attempted to do what they advised us, but of direction, the rest of the family had no concept of what they have been to do. They didn't understand contingencies and reinforcement.

As I grew older, I became an increasing number of chargeable for each person. How I hated coming home from school. I knew I could need to be everybody's nursemaid. I had buddies at college, however, I never saw all people out of doors of the school. I truly never had a chum over to the house. The few times I went to visit different youngsters at their houses have been painful. I hated seeing how everyday people lived. I hated seeing dad and mom running a home as opposed to a kid. I hated seeing neat, clean residences. I hated seeing mothers coming domestic with their fingers full of baggage once they shopped.

In ninth grade, there has been a lady named Isadora who tried to get near me. She had a single mom who turned into the final hippie as you could likely tell from Isadora's name. She changed into named after the dancer Isadora Duncan. Her mother turned into a wannabe dancer who made her living as a waitress at a famous community diner so everybody knew her. I went over to their rental perhaps five or six times. It became almost as dirty as ours, but in a beatnik cluttered way. Her mother might show videotapes of Isadora Duncan dancing and we might all dance along. That's the extent of my dance lessons. I surely changed into a klutz. I nevertheless can't dance.

They knew approximately my circle of relatives. I suppose from the neighborhood gossip that her mom picked up on the diner. Her mom tried to get me to talk about my circle of relatives and became always asking if she could help out in any way. I knew she was seeking to be quality, but I couldn't take delivery of it. There turned into additionally every other problem. Isadora turned into a boy loopy and become equipped for intercourse at fourteen. I wasn't even prepared for sex at twenty-two. All she desired to talk about changed into boys and sex and all I desired to speak approximately become books I examine. I had truly no interest in boys and sex. I loved analyzing approximately intercourse in books like East of Eden, however, my hobby turned into vicarious. I sincerely turned into odd for a fourteen-year-old lady. I just couldn't receive something those fine people had to provide. I stopped seeing Isadora and stopped going to her condominium. My only touch along with her after that was writing approximately her whilst she did inside the high faculty musicals. I assume she became appropriate. I don't recognize it. I never went to any of the musicals.

One of the reasons I did so properly at college became that

way wherein I changed into the happiest. I loved school. I cherished my instructors. I cherished getting to know. I cherished the usage of my mind. I loved the success I executed there. The school was the simplest area in which I was given advantageous reinforcement for who I changed into and who I become at college became now not the same as who I became at home. I think returning to how I turned into continually smiling in faculty. Everyone concept that I become the happiest, sweetest girl, however, I become a Jekyll and Hyde lady. At home, I never smiled. No one smiled. I changed into a robotic doing what I needed to do.

I in no way did more-curricular stuff until high faculty. I was a great athlete, but couldn't be part of any groups. I might have cherished having joined Scouts, however, that was out of the query. I couldn't visit conferences. My mother and father additionally stated that we didn't have cash for a uniform. My mother and father and grandparents always stated that I changed into wished at home.

As a freshman, I stood as much as my dad and mom for the primary time. I insisted that I be allowed to stay after school with the opposite children. That turned into my first step toward leaving home. I labored on the faculty paper. That has become my haven. I cherished the children at the staff. They mentioned highbrow things that I had no idea existed within the real international, like nuclear disarmament, worldwide warming, and gay rights. They examine Time mag. I thought that turned into the maximum highbrow magazine in the global. Every week I would get the maximum latest trouble from the college library and study it from cover to cover. To me, Time represented a thinking man or woman's bible. It represented what I desired to be intellectual. When I changed into a senior, I have become the editor-in-leader of the paper. Those had been my happiest memories of high college, bringing out the newspaper each week."

Abra pictured the troubles of the newspaper, the Tribune. She might examine each article over and over. She knew about every occasion that took place at college. She knew approximately the football games, track meets, technological know-how gala's, and dances, but she by no means attended any of them. She loved the editorial personnel meetings whilst the kids talked about world affairs or what became happening regionally. They added her to the arena outdoor of Seventeenth Street and York High School.

"As I was given older, my grandparents commenced speaking about plans for the future when they were gone. Neither of them had graduated from high faculty. They had been too bad and needed to visit work early on. They wanted me to go to Queens College and end up a trainer. To them, that became like going to Harvard and turning into a medical doctor. Then I may want to get a great job with plenty of time off so I could take care of my own family the relaxation of our lives. I bear in mind them pronouncing that I had to be responsible for everybody for the relaxation of my existence. They'd say, Abra, you need to be the top of this own family while we're lifeless. I changed into fourteen and they were laying out my life for me all the manner to my grave. I knew that I needed to getaway. I couldn't be shackled to those human beings and waste my life. I had goals and they weren't to attend to my family. I have desired to be an unbiased professional woman who might wear lovable garments and travel and have sophisticated buddies and live in a lovely rental. Anything however dwelling at home with the Ginzbergs.

We lived in a big apartment building. Our rental changed within the return of the construction. It became U fashioned and you had to walk through an extended courtyard to get to our front. There become a massive hallway with mailboxes and doorbells. You needed to be buzzed up, but the door became generally propped open. We lived in 2F on the second ground. Up to two flights of unlit stairs on thread-naked carpeting. We had a three-bedroom apartment with one restroom. My dad and mom had one bedroom, Rachel and Noah shared one, and I had a tiny bedroom that become my refuge. The condominium by no means was given any solar. It changed into usually darkish. That's how I don't forget it, dark and crowded with people and fixtures. I don't realize why we lived on the second ground while my parents couldn't negotiate the stairs. Why didn't they pass down to a first ground condo? Maybe that turned into one of the reasons they did not often leave the apartment.

We lived on my mother and father's disability assessments and the money that both sets of grandparents gave us. My mother's mother and father were rarely around, however, they gave us money often. They lived in Florida and came up to New York once twelve months. My dad's dad and mom saved their own family going. They labored for the town of New York doing menial jobs. They didn't make tons of money, however, they'd job safety which to them changed into the most crucial factor about an activity. My father become the simplest infant and my mom's brother had died so there had been no uncles or aunts to help out.

It became simply our satisfied little nuclear own family with two units of grandparents.

The kids had been in special education lessons and had been continuously going to medical doctors. They had masses of fitness troubles. Rachel became allergic to the whole thing and was covered with rashes and become continually sneezing and wheezing. Noah had petit malls and it became difficult to find the proper meds for him, however, ultimately they had been pretty well controlled. There have been always social employees and nurses coming to the residence. As I got older, I took on extra family obligations. I crammed out forms, talked to the social people and psychologists and instructors, and all the individuals who got us via existence. I don't forget early on to read the mental and clinical reports on Rachel and Noah. My SAT vocabulary stepped forward fantastically from the reports. I found words like idiopathic, noncompliant, and dysfunctional. Words that weren't a part of an excessive college children's vocabulary.

You realize, now we've got so many children in the colleges who do the identical for his or her dad and mom who don't speak English. We have those little children going with their dad and mom to the doctor and translating their mother and father's illnesses. I functioned quite an awful lot the equal way, simplest it wasn't due to the fact my parents and siblings couldn't talk English. It turned into due to the fact they were too cognitively constrained to cope with the outside international. I turned into the extraordinary communicator."

She recalled the looks of condescension, abhorrence, and generally pity that the outside world gave her once they found out how cognitively impaired her circle of relatives become. She unsuccessfully tried to overlook an especially humiliating revel she had while she took Miriam to the physician. Cynical, bitter Dr. Weisberg was in the circle of relatives and health practitioners. He turned into fats and had those hairy grey eyebrows that partially blanketed his eyes. He reeked of cigarette smoke and had cigarette ashes scattered across his chest. Even in those days, doctors knew that smoking become lethal, however, Dr. Weisberg couldn't heed the recommendation, "doctor, heal thyself."

On one of the many trips she made together with her mother to Dr. Weisberg, he requested with exasperation, "What's wrong along with her now?" He did not look at Miriam. He is in no way looking at Miriam. He addressed Abra as though she have been the parent and Miriam the child.

Abra spoke back, "She says that it hurts whilst she pees and on occasion, there's blood in her pee."

Dr. Weisberg requested, "How often does she urinate?" She translated for her mother, "How frequently do you pee?" "A lot." Abra said, "But how tons?"

Abra couldn't make Miriam recognize that Dr. Weisberg desired a selected number of times in a time frame. He tested Miriam vaginally even as twelve-year-old Abra cowered in a nook seeking to appear everywhere but at her mom's exposed vagina. She recalled the tears trickling down her cheeks and her resolving to forestall them so no person would see her disgrace for Miriam and herself. After poking around, Dr. Weisberg concluded, "It's probable some other bladder contamination. Take this cup and feature her urinate in it. Then give it to the nurse. I suppose she gets those bladder infections because she wipes from again to front rather than front to again. She receives shit in her vagina. I'm no longer certain she even wipes. Teach her how to wipe when she pees. She desires to preserve herself cleanser. Tell her to take a tub more regularly. She's a schmutz. Like an animal. Fey." He shook his head as he regarded away in disgust. This turned into a health practitioner saying that her mother was grimy like an animal. How she despised him. She desired to scream in his face. "You're the animal. You're a doctor. You're presupposed to deal with human beings well." But on the path, she changed into silence.

Abra took Miriam to the toilet and told her to pee inside the cup. She couldn't manage it so Abra held the cup and watched with horror as Miriam's urine-soaked her fingers. Abra carefully washed her arms after which used three disinfectant packets to meticulously cleanse each inch of the pores and skin on her arms. She washed the doors of the cup and took it to the nurse. Teaching her mother away to wipe, become the intensity of humiliation. She couldn't proportion this revel in with Beth; it was too painful to verbalize this bad event to each person.

"My grandparents have been schooling me to run the circle of relatives once they became infirmed or died. They wanted me to take care of my circle of relatives for the rest of my life. They have been constantly saying, 'When we die, you need to be answerable for the circle of relatives. You're the only one that can try this. When you're at work, you'll rent someone to live in the residence to take care of all of us.' This curse hung over me. I notion of it continuously. I thought of how I would escape. I wanted a life for myself. I didn't want to be unselfish and devote my life to my own family. There's the phrase – unselfish. I'm the primary to confess that I'm egocentric. I placed myself before my circle of relatives. If I hadn't, I suppose I would have dedicated suicide or come to be a robot, just dwelling daily without wondering or feeling anything. My existence would have been a waste, a total and whole waste of a life."

After the 0.33 cup of coffee, Abra stated, "I'm all talked out. I can't talk anymore. Well, what do you think? Do you watch I'm a merciless, egocentric person for running away from my circle of relatives, for leaving them to fend for themselves? I knew that so long as my grandparents had been alive, they would help, however seeing that they died I have no idea who helped them. They made it. The youngsters had been in institution homes so they weren't with Jacob and Miriam. Thank God. I noticed that their home address was specific. Somehow they moved from Queens to somewhere in Brooklyn. I assume from the deal that they're close to the seaside. They made it without me. That at the least makes me sense better. It confirms that I made the right decision. Beth, did you watch any of this? Did you know?"

"Yes. I knew your dad and mom weren't dead because a variety of times you referred to them inside the present aggravating. Once at the seaside you stated my father IS a smoker, now not WAS a smoker. Another time you said my mom loves Oprah. She's God to her. I knew you didn't need to speak about them so I didn't assign you. I so desired to have you share your past with me. It harms which you didn't.

I had no concept you had a brother and sister. That's quite a wonder. Abra, your tale has modified how I see you and I'm not positive what the photo is. I usually checked out you as a girl of a thriller. You exuded this feeling of the unique because I knew there had been secrets that you had. But permit me to ask you the apparent question, did you emerge as a psychologist due to all this?"

Abra nodded her head. "I've thought about this question for years. Yeah, I'm certain a part of the motive I went into psych become because of my family, but there's more. I suppose I naively notion that I would be capable of recognizing myself if I have become a psychologist and greater importantly get validation for the choice I made to depart." "Did you?"

"Well, I assume my education helped me understand myself better, but it hasn't helped me with the ethical trouble. That's a distinctive ballpark. Did I do the proper aspect then? Should I have finished something for them beyond 16 years? I still don't have convincing answers."

Beth said, "How about the retardation? Is it genetic? Have your remote the feasible syndrome?" Abra spoke back, "It needs to be genetic. When I learned approximately genetics in excessive faculty, I got here to the belief that the Ginzberg circle of relatives had dirty genes. Over the years, I've checked into different viable syndromes. I've never determined one that fits their traits. Up to the time I left, there hadn't been any genetic studies of the own family. There may additionally be a few due to the fact I left however I seriously doubt it. They wouldn't apprehend genetics and could never cooperate with any trying out. You know we Jews have masses of genetic glitches like Tay Sachs. But it's not any of those. Maybe it's all that inbreeding over the centuries of living in ghettos."

Beth leaned ahead and requested, "The obvious question is have you ever been examined genetically?" "Never and won't. I will never have children so it's no longer a difficulty." "Let me psychologize. I assume your circle of relatives history explains why you've in no way had a long-lasting date with a man. God best is aware of, you've had so many probabilities, however, you've always ended a dating whilst it got extreme. Remember David? He was perfect for you and crazy approximately you, but you suddenly stopped seeing him. You by no means truly came up with a motive for doing that. Now I recognize why."

Abra nervously requested, "Do you suspect less of me now which you realize?" Beth grabbed Abra's hands and held them tightly. "No, I think greater of you. I can't believe living the existence you probably did. I grew up in a glad, loving home so I can't begin to understand what you went thru. I have no idea what I might have carried out, but I suppose I could have done what you probably did."

They paid the bill and left the eating place. It became a heat, starry night time so they walked arm in arm along the water at Battery Park. The full moon created trails of rippled water. They regarded out at Fort Sumter marveling at the tranquility of this nighttime in comparison to a night over one hundred years ago whilst the Civil War capturing started. They made idle chatter about the weather, the city, Clay's development in kindergarten, and Beth and Tom's attempts to adopt a child. Suddenly they found out how tired they had been and headed returned to the hotel. When they again to their room, Beth stated, "Tell me approximately Miss B. It's funny. I've in no way been in a position to name her Edith either."

Abra cherished talking about Edith Benjamin because she got her out of F Street. She aided and abetted her break out to the real global. Without her, Abra possibly would have remained with the Ginzberg circle of relatives, at the least for some time until she changed into able to get away on her very own.

"Ah - Edith Benjamin - my savior! She turned into my freshman English instructor. Some of the children made fun of her because she became unattractive, however the clever kids fashionable her because she was a charismatic trainer who instilled a love of literature in us. I adored her magnificence and could loaf around her every time I had a risk. She shared special books with me. She delivered me to Catcher in the Rye and East of Eden. When the first figure-trainer night become coming near, she told me that she was eager to satisfy my dad and mom and tell them what first-rate thoughts I had. I had by no means instructed absolutely everyone approximately my dad and mom although many people knew. I instructed her they weren't coming. She requested why and I broke down and instructed her all approximately my circle of relatives. She changed into the handiest character I unfolded into in my first 18 years of existence. Come to think of it she's the simplest man or woman until now that I ever completely spread out to. She became my conspirator in hiding the gory info of my domestic life. There are masses to tell about incredible Edith Benjamin, however, I'll keep it for yet again. I'm concerned approximately her. She has very excessive blood stress and medication isn't bringing it down. I communicate with her almost every day. She says she's doing nice, however I ought to go to her and spot for myself.

She nevertheless lives in that excellent old apartment in Manhattan. Beth, do you recall that remarkable Christmas excursion while we went as much as New York City and stayed with her? There became a blizzard and we have been snowed in her rental. New York City changed into completely paralyzed. We had so much amusement with her. Remember that day we stayed in our pajamas all day and attempted to study all the titles of the books in her library. The next day we went out inside the snow and made angels within the snow in Riverside Park.

We want to find time to talk and speak and speak sometime soon. We're each so tired and you have to take off early and I'm having brunch with the Nelsons."

Beth got into her nightgown and jumped into the mattress. "I have best one more query to invite you. How do you feel approximately Rachel's death?" Abra turned into setting on her sweats and said, "I don't recognize. It's going to take me a while to procedure how I feel. I did love her, however, I loved myself greater than her. I don't know if I feel any grief. I do realize I experience the comfort that certainly one of my wards is now not haunting me. I ought to sense guilty about feeling remedy, however, I don't. More than anything, I sense fear that humans will find out about me. That overwhelming fear haunts me extra than ever. As you thoroughly know, I'm a secretive person and I don't need my secrets to be made public. I don't want to be ousted.

Hopefully, when I come to your vicinity at Thanksgiving we'll find a while to speak approximately that. I'll use that as my homework venture. I'll carry Godiva chocolates and an answer to your query. And perhaps via you, they'll get an infant. I wish so Beth. You need to have masses of toddlers. You and Tom have so much love to give. I sense horrible that we haven't talked about your adoption plans." At her last go to with Beth and Tom all through the summertime, they had disclosed that they couldn't have any extra children. They weren't positive why no matter all of the trying out they had subjected themselves to. There become a low sperm remember for Tom and lots of fibroid tumors for Beth. But whatever the reasons, they have been determined to have more children. Since not one of the current miracles of drugs was fantastic for them, they have been going to undertake. They had registered with different agencies and have been vetted. Now they have been looking forward to the kid who could entire their own family.

"There's nothing to speak about proper now. We've determined now not to do a foreign adoption. We have so many children who want a domestic here in America I don't think we must journey the sector to discover a kid. We may additionally adopt a biracial or handicapped kid or a biracial and handicapped child. There are lots to be had. Nobody wants them. I recognize you likely don't apprehend how we may want to are trying to find out a handicapped youngster while you ran far from such kids, but we want to proportion our love with a kid who others find tough to love."

"Knowing you, I apprehend. You and Tom are incredible humans. I ought to by no means in a million years do what you're doing however if absolutely everyone can, it's you two. Maybe after I see you at Thanksgiving, there might be some other Newland in your house. I wish so. Whatever makes it viable so that it will love this type of child made it viable on the way to love me. I wasn't too exclusive from a handicapped youngster whilst we met. I changed into desperately in need of someone to like and educate me approximately the world. That someone becomes you. For a few lucky children, a good way to be you once more." They kissed goodnight and fell asleep at once.

CHAPTER FIVE

Beth and Abra popped out of bed at 6 AM, a lot as they'd completed during their four years at Jackson. With a quick shower and a cursory comb via her matted hair, Beth turned out the door and was in her vehicle by 6:30 keen to force home to Richmond to her loved Tim and Clay. Beth checked out with the aid of 7:30 and waited in the front of the hotel for Pete Nelson to choose her up. She breathed within the candy humid morning air as she eyed the still snoozing streets of Charleston affected by Saturday night's debris.

During her years in South Carolina Abra mastered her career. During her three years of Grad College in Columbia, she discovered the content material of psychology, and at some point during her year internship in Charleston, she carried out what she had learned in the actual world. She enjoyed her time at Columbia doing what she did best, faculty. She had a restrained social life, except for 4 months in her second year of grad faculty whilst she took a path in intercourse training from a neighbor. One afternoon as she became analyzing her condo, she spoke back to a knock at the door to find the man who lived next door.

"Hi, I'm Drew Ellis. I stay around the corner. I forgot my keys and my roommates are out. Can I use your balcony to get to my area?"

Although Drew gave the impression of ninety percent of the guys on campus, Abra had noticed him because he always wore a baseball cap backward. In reality, she silently mentioned him as Backwards. He turned into one of the many university college students who wore the college uniform of a tee blouse on a warm day or a sweatshirt on a cold day, denim, sloppy footwear, or turn flops. "Sure, simply don't fall. I can't manage to pay for to be sued."

Like a trapeze artist, he agilely leaped from her balcony to his and disappeared into his apartment. A short while later, he got here to her door with beers as a thank you present. In the next few hours, he advised her of his complete existence story. All he wanted to do became to explore the world, however, he promised his mom he would graduate from university so he became biding his time until he graduated in May. After high faculty, he spent a year backpacking via South America, and after his sophomore twelve months, he took twelve months off to travel through Eastern Europe. He became a journalism major with aspirations of being a foreign correspondent or a travel author. Over the subsequent three weeks, he shared the writings of his travels with Abra, who vicariously visited Machu Pichu and canoed up the Amazon. When Drew talked of his adventures, Abra listened to him as if he were Marco Polo sharing his travels in China. One day several weeks after his balcony stunt, he said, "Abra, I genuinely like you. Let's have sex."

She laughed. "Just like that? Drew, I like you too, but I'm now not sure that we should do it just due to the fact we like each other. There are several human beings I like but I don't sleep with them. Anyhow, might you accept as true with that this twenty-three-year-old best had intercourse once and it became a fiasco so I'm a chunk leery of a second strive?"

"Abra, I'm no notable lover. I simply revel in intercourse. Give me a chance and maybe I can get you to revel in it too." And he did. For four months before he graduated, they had fun sex. Drew became no longer making plans on attending graduation so whilst he finished his final, he came to mention goodbye to Abra. He changed into off to China for any other adventure and he or she turned into returned to her ordinary life of analyzing. She could omit his sweetness and the comfort of no-ties intercourse. He turned into a true loose spirit. She had never regarded absolutely everyone like him before or seen that. Everyone she met in college and after school became targeted in a profession and eventual marriage and kids. He had an open-ended future. Over the years, she googled his call to look if he had come to be a travel writer or a journalist, however, she in no way determined any reference to him. He disappeared into the world.

Her year in Charleston turned into one-of-a-kind from her time in Columbia. It became much less cerebral and more action stuffed as she started work as a psychologist, and it became gratifying as she got here to the realization that she had decided on the right profession. And the year brought deep friendships, with Martha, Pete, and her roommate, Judy.

As Director of Psychological Services for the Wando Schools, Martha Nelson supervised Abra's college psych internship. She expertly molded Abra's abilities in designing and applying remedy plans for bothered kids and administering and decoding exams to reach diagnoses related to suitable offerings. Pete becomes an artwork teacher at Wando High School wherein Abra becomes primarily based. Although she could have cherished Pete for being Martha's husband, she found out to like him for being an all-giving husband, father, and buddy. It changed into her first revel in having a man, and a married guy at that, as a pal.

Martha and Peter looked like they stepped off a page of an advert for dwelling on the good life in Sweden, with their thin blond hair, blue eyes, faded pores and skin, and lanky builds. At school, Martha dressed conservatively, but at domestic she reverted to the hippie garb of her children. She wore gauzy off-the-shoulder blouses, without a bra, lengthy multicolored skirts, and, of the route, Birkenstocks. She held her hair up with amber sticks which stuck out at steep angles and had been risky to everyone getting too close. Ironically, she changed into always hugging people who needed to keep away from being impaled via the sticks. Initially, Abra turned into intimidated by using their Nordic appearance and her expectation that they might personify the stereotypical aloof personalities of Scandinavians. But she fast revised her expectancies as she found them to be outgoing and warm.

Martha and Pete have been transplanted from Iowa. They met in university in the course of their hippie phase. Upon graduating, they married and then spent six months using the states, way to a small inheritance from Martha's grandmother. When they visited Charleston, they instantly knew they observed the vicinity they desired to name domestic. So they moved to Columbia where Martha enrolled in the psych software at the University of South Carolina and Pete entered the grasp of the pleasant arts program. After they finished Grad College, they moved to the Charleston place where Martha have become a psychologist for the Wando Schools and Pete an artwork instructor at Wando High School.

While they have been in grad school, they often visited Charleston and located nearby Sullivan Island, a tiny island that bravely confronted the effective Atlantic Ocean at the east, whilst being sponsored up via the calm Intracoastal Waterway at the west. Coming from the land-locked Midwest, they were enchanted via the expanse of the ocean, the in no way ending horizon, the best whiteness of the sand, and the swooping pelicans. All of their spare time became spent exploring the beach that was deserted while the vacationers weren't around, and semi-abandoned even when the tourists had been.

Their love of Sullivan Island was fed not best by using its splendor, but its morbid history. The palm-coated streets of Sullivan Island belied its sinister past. This becomes the drop-off point for slaves on their voyages from Africa to the markets in Charleston. Strewn on the beaches were reminiscences of America's ugly beyond as despoilers of black lives. To add even greater spice to the island's history turned into the fact that Edgar Allen Poe was based totally at a navy put up there when he became young. He can also have even used the island as the prototype for the island in his e-book, The Gold Bug. Edgar Allen Poe, the grasp of the macabre, solid diabolical shadows on sunny Sullivan Island. And then there was the haunting of the island by the eight crew contributors of the Hunley, the most effective submarine used inside the Civil War, which sank off the island on its maiden voyage.

Abra was satisfied to be spending the day with the Nelsons. She desired to purge herself from the ultimate night's painful disclosure to Beth. She knew that ultimately she could inform the Nelsons, but today she desired to overlook herself and think simplest about them and their great shared past. She was dissatisfied that she wouldn't see their twins who were away at college. Eric became on the University of South Carolina majoring in fraternity and enterprise, even as Lisa become on the Savannah School of Art following in her father's footsteps majoring in art.

As Abra waited at the lodge for Pete to pick out her up, she reflected on how her lifestyles intersected with the Nelson's. Abra and Judy had each obtained internships in the Charleston region, Abra with the Wando Schools and Judy with the Charleston City Schools. They decided that because they had lived together amicably for three years of Grad College, they could keep for any other twelve months. After her interview with Martha approximately her obligations as an intern, Abra requested if she knew of a rental that she and Judy would possibly lease. She cited that Judy was black and requested if that would be a trouble because Abra was nicely privy to housing discrimination against blacks in the South, as well as in the North. Martha said, "I own an antique house on Sullivan Island no longer a long way from my house. It's no longer inside the pleasant circumstance, but it's close to the seashore and also you both should get to paintings without difficulty. Come see it. And in case you don't find it irresistible, it received hurt my feelings. And the quality of all, it's reasonably priced! And I don't care if Judy is black or crimson as long as she will pay the hire. She's a psychologist so she should be an awesome person."

Abra spoke back, "We're grad students who've lived in a slum the past three years. Anything may be a development.

And you probably did say the magic phrase – cheap." The next day Abra and Judy met Martha at the house and they noticed that it turned into a fixer-top and not a good deal of development over wherein they had been living for the beyond three years, however, it had one asset – it turned into one block from the seashore. Martha and Peter offered the residence to Martha's father after her mother died. They wanted him close to them, but he didn't like being far away from Iowa and his buddies. He spent the maximum of his time touring again to Iowa and by no means was given round to creating any of the desperately needed maintenance at the house. After a few years, he moved back to Iowa permanently so that they had this residence which because of its cheap charge, they without difficulty rented to tourists in the summers, however, was vacant during the relaxation of the twelve months and changed into an ideal for Abra and Judy's wishes.

Abra and Judy spent numerous weekends cleaning the residence, but it in reality wished a year for the task to be finished. Still, they cherished the residence: its dank odor which resisted all tries at being neutralized by using incense, scented candles, and room deodorizers; its screened porch dotted with holes free admission of mosquitoes eager to feast on human blood; and its endless parade of cockroaches, or greater euphemistically, palmetto bugs, marching thru the kitchen, the bathroom, and every spot within the house wherein they ruled ultimate despite consistent barrages of bug spray. But maximum of all they cherished the beach which they walked or jogged whenever their tight schedules allowed.

The sturdy bond between Abra and Martha began with Ella, a student Martha assigned to Abra for counseling.

Ella, a Wando High School sophomore, proved to be the hardest pupil Abra could work with during her internship. Ella, known as the school slut inclined and eager to sleep with each person, defied authority figures, refused to do faculty paintings, become truant, and engaged in self-abusive conduct. Most troubling, she was a cutter.

Abra was surprised when she met Ella. She had studied her document and predicted a big, loud youngster-ager. Instead, she found a tiny, rail-skinny lady who regarded herself as if she had been in fundamental school except for her breast buds which she proudly showed off via no longer sporting a bra below her tight brief tee shirts. She had a pretty face with ideal features, however, it appeared clown-like because of the heavy make-up Ella haphazardly carried out. Her long, stringy hair included the multitude of jewelry lining both ears. She used her twig-like hands as dartboards for all forms of sharp gadgets. She seemed proud of this self-mutilation and by no means tried to cover her arms. When she spoke, her voice was candy and childlike, but the phrases she spoke have been those of a jaded female who had visible the worst of lifestyles.

Ella got here from a poor, dysfunctional home so there was no cash for psychiatric help, even though there was money for alcohol and capsules. Ella's father was a small-time drug dealer and her mom an occasional hooker, however, due to her meth dependency she had misplaced her enamel and turned into skeletal, making her appealing to only the maximum sexually desperate. Surprisingly Ella didn't drink or do capsules, perhaps because she knew first-hand the harm those insidious killers wreaked on her dad and mom. Over the ultimate ten years, Ella had periodically been removed from the home while someone became arrested or came to the attention of the authorities. She was placed in foster houses that had been as dysfunctional as her domestic and returned to her mother and father because there has been no area else for her.

Abra's newly emerging counseling skills have been all that Ella changed into going to get inside the manner of mental assistance. They met two times per week for communication therapy. No one had ever been interested in Ella earlier, particularly a pretty younger girl so Ella lapped up the eye from Abra and spread out approximately her drug-addicted dad and mom and their lengthy records of dependence on welfare and criminal activities. She freely mentioned her need for intercourse and her belief that it would provide a manner out of her life with her mother and father. She said that she changed into an extremely good fuck and that changed into why all the guys in college cherished her. She bragged that she might do as many as three men at one time. It became difficult to believe that she thought that those boys cherished her, but she needed to consider this, or she could need to understand that she turned into a throw-away sex object. Abra was bowled over by the brilliant description of sex that Ella proudly supplied, but she turned carefully to mask her surprise and abhorrence. This changed into her first experience with a child who became performing out sexually and it became enlightening for Abra who up to now had "conventional" intercourse with handiest Rick and Drew. In their complying with-up assembly after Abra's first session with Ella, Martha recommended Abra to set limits on the subjects and language she allowed Ella to apply in their periods because they were inside the college placing. Ella loved describing the only component she idea she become good at – intercourse but reluctantly agreed no longer to talk about it. She also agreed that she could not use the words, fuck or shit, the most regularly used phrases in her restrained vocabulary.

At their second consultation, Ella methodically described each of the self-inflicted wounds on her hands. "Sticking matters in my palms hurts simplest a bit. It's sufficient to make me no longer need to harm myself plenty. It continues me from killing myself. Sometimes I think of stabbing a knife into my chest, however, rather than stick it into my arm It's like I'm a balloon full of air and once I reduce myself I allow a bit of the air out. I don't sense so wound up and tight anymore." She pointed to sores that she made with pins, knives, and needles indicating the specific styles they made. Because she became right exceeded, her left arm become a patchwork of sores with diverse degrees of scabbing. Abra and Martha had determined that this will be the first area that Abra need to recognition on. Ella agreed to stop the cutting and signed a settlement formalizing her decision. They developed a list of behaviors that Ella would use whenever she felt like hurting herself. The behavior that Ella appreciated first-rate turned into screaming all of the grimy phrases she should think about, however, best if she turned into a non-public location. If she was in a public vicinity, like school, she turned to jot these phrases with the usage of massive letters. Abra informed Ella's instructors about this so that they might now not punish Ella if they located the written profanity. Even if they saw the various phrases Ella wrote, they likely wouldn't be able to read them because of Ella's negative spelling and handwriting, even though fuck and shit have been usually spelled effectively. Abra marveled as the sores on Ella's arm started to fade. Abra and Martha were recommended for this change in Ella's behavior. They decided to subsequently focus on enhancing her attendance. Since Abra and Ella had started assembly on Tuesdays and Thursdays, Ella had not overlooked in recent times of school. Now they centered on the opposite three days of the week.

Abra became desperate to find something, except intercourse, that made Ella's experience suitable. She discovered that Ella liked the handiest one elegance - her artwork elegance with Pete. Abra talked to Pete and Martha about how they might use art to assist Ella. Pete guided Ella as she created watercolor seaside scenes. Ella turned transformed whilst she drew. She expressed the passion and pain in her soul with robust bold brush strokes. As she painted, she talked and ranted about her dad and mom and the bias of her life. "Why is there such ugliness in my lifestyle whilst there's such beauty in the world? Why can't my existence be like the seashore — stunning and quiet? Instead of filthy and disgusting and screwed up. Just like me." Her artwork was pretty top artistically, however, what made them unique turned into the emotion she expressed with harsh, vibrant colors.

After eight weeks of counseling, Martha invited Ella and Abra to her home for a Sunday lunch observed using a portray session on the beach with Pete. The house, a block from the seaside, changed into gray shingled and had a wrap-round porch with rockers, Abra's favored form of chair. At Jackson, she had rocked on her dorm porch so often she was sure that she had etched permanent ruts on the porch floorboards. In the dwelling room, a ceiling fan continuously circulated overhead blowing the sheer curtains out the windows onto the porch rockers. The living room walls were covered with Pete's oil paintings of the seashore and the twins at various stages in their early life. The non-public series of nude drawings of Martha turned stored in Martha and Pete's bedroom, away from the eyes of informal traffic.

The breeze from the fan carried the scent of shrimp and pasta that Martha had cooked along with strawberry cobbler crafted from berries the kids had picked. That mingled with the odor of floor coffee beans made Abra salivate like Pavlov's dog every time she recalled that first meal at the Nelson's.

Abra and Ella had been each received over via those heat humans and their soft animals. Here become an instance of a loving marriage and happy children, something Abra hadn't visible in her first eighteen years of existence or within the households she labored within her expert training. For the primary time, Ella witnessed a glad circle of relatives. Seeing a satisfied circle of relatives in the movies or on TV didn't depend. That was make-consider. This changed into real.

After lunch, Pete and Ella took their portray materials to the beach. Abra and Martha took an extended stroll whilst the children and dogs romped in the ocean. The moist puppies rolled within the sand and covered every person inside five feet with sticky sand that refused to clean off even in the salty ocean. Ella stopped portraying and wildly chased the dogs as they ran in circles. Then she rolled inside the sand as she laughed from the depths of her soul, something Abra had by no means seen her do and maybe she had never achieved before. After an hour, the artists packed up their substances and went back to the house so that they may display to the others what they'd produced. Ella painted a serene ocean with two distant figures taking walks alongside the seaside, Abra, and Martha. She offered it to Abra as a gift for assisting her. "Miss Berg, I need you to have this photograph due to the fact you've helped me a lot. Thanks for making my experience better." Abra was triumphant over with emotion and happiness that she had made a difference in Ella's life. Here become proof that she had picked the right profession. She became intended to be a helper, a supporter, and a nurturer.

Later when Abra drove Ella home, Ella mournfully cried. "That's the existence I want. Miss Berg. I want to house like Dr. Nelson's. I want pleasant fixtures. I want to be with the best people. Help me get away from my family. I want to break out and stay with a normal lifestyle or I'll die. Can I come and live with you? I could be your youngster. You could adopt me. Or I might be your little sister. Please. Please. I'm going to die if I should live with those shits. I hate my existence. I need a lifelike those humans have."

Abra become so conquered by way of this outburst, that she couldn't force herself. She pulled over to the aspect of the street frantically groping for the right phrases that an excellent psychologist might use. Here turned into Ella asking Abra to be her Miss Benjamin. But she couldn't. She didn't have the money or the felony assistance to take Ella. And Ella didn't have whatever that could make her a success although she did escape. She hadn't benefited from school so she was poorly knowledgeable. She should barely examine and write. She probably would have trouble making it at a network university even if she eventually completed excessive school. And she didn't have any job abilities. It wouldn't be paintings even if Abra desired to do it. But Abra knew wherein the uncrossable line between being a professional and being a friend started and ended. She also knew the truth about Ella – she couldn't climb out of her quagmire irrespective of what Abra would possibly do.

In a quavering voice, Abra stated, "Ella, you know I want that will help you, however, I can't take you in. I'll have social offerings take you away from your mother and father. They'll discover a precise foster domestic for you. I promise."

Ella's voice reeked of bitterness, "Oh yeah, that would assist. Who might need me as a foster child? I've been in foster houses one million instances in view that I was a child. I've been screwed and beaten with the aid of weirdoes and perverts. Forget it. They'd send me to a group in which I'd discover ways to whore and deal. No, thank you. That's now not what I had in my thoughts. I desire I'd never met you or Nelson. I don't want to know what's out there that I can't have. I don't need to peer you anymore. Let's go. Take me returned to my shithole to see my dad and mom popping up and fucking. Maybe my father will want to do me. I might be geared up for that now."

Abra changed into desperate. She couldn't think of what to do. Frantically, she said, "Wait. Wait. Wait. Let's communicate to Dr. Nelson approximately this. Let's see what she will do to assist. Ella, I'm simply beginning out as a psychologist. I don't know all the options for you. Please let me help you."

Ella fiercely yelled, "How will you assist me? Put my lower back within the gadget? Put me on the streets? Take me domestic or I'll walk." Abra drove the rest of the way to Ella's trailer silently crying even as Ella jiggled up and down as though she had been going to blow up. Her proper hand started out gouging her left arm marking the cancellation of the self-mutilation settlement. As soon as she stopped at Ella's trailer, Ella grabbed the painting she had given Abra and tore it up. She glared at Abra as she threw the portions at her. Then she ran out of Abra's lifestyle all the time.

Abra slowly drove back to the Nelsons afraid she might crash because of her blinding tears. When she was given to their house, she sat in the automobile and cried uncontrollably. Cried because she couldn't help Ella. Cried because of the life Ella become doomed to. Cried because she doubted if she became surely going to be a terrific psychologist despite everything.

Eric become shooting baskets within the driveway whilst he observed Abra. He approached the automobile and cautiously asked, "Abra, what's the problem? Come inside the house." Abra couldn't forestall crying so Eric bumped into the residence for Martha. Martha came out to the car and was given in. "Cry all you want. When you're finished tell me what occurred."

Abra babbled incoherently, but gradually Martha became able to piece collectively what had happened in the thirty minutes for the reason that she had left. Thirty minutes changed Abra in such a lot of ways. Martha took Abra's hand and said, "You're gaining knowledge of a lesson that I need to preserve studying myself. We can't save the world via ourselves. We can't give youngsters like Ella a flavor of what existence ought to be like and anticipate them to alternate on their very own. We want to get a child like her earlier and get social services worried. She must were taken from that hellhole permanently for a long term in the past. She wanted special schooling, remedy, and a maximum of all a supportive domestic with affection. We gave her a glimpse of what lifestyles will be like and she or he wanted it. Were we foolish to contain her in our lives? Were we right to allow her hope? I don't recognize it. I thought it'd assist her, in particular, once you stopped her self-abusive behavior. We're each do-gooder at heart. We suppose we will store the sector. But we will do it by myself. We can most effectively do a little bit and if there are enough folks who do their little bits collectively perhaps we can save extra youngsters. But Abra, don't question your capability to be an amazing psychologist. I've worked with such a lot of interns and you're one of the pleasant. One day you'll be a great psychologist, however, you'll nevertheless lose youngsters like Ella. It'll ruin your coronary heart, however, you need to maintain going for the children you can assist."

They talked for two hours. Martha switched from mentor to pal and lower back once more. By the time Abra left, she changed into a calmer, but she still couldn't accept that there has been nothing they may do for Ella. Abra went back to the cottage and advised Judy approximately what had occurred and they talked until bedtime. After that, Abra lay in bed and talked to herself. She as compared her domestic to Ella's. She knew her home was bad, but now not as compared to Ella's. There had been no drugs or booze or sex in her house. She knew she turned into so fortunate that she had the method to break out, her brains and Miss Benjamin. She felt an awesome sadness understanding that Ella could by no means get away. She kept whispering into her pillow. "Forgive me, Ella. I wanted that will help you. I couldn't take you. Please, please forgive me"

Ella never backs to school. She ran far away from home with a boy, additionally an excessive college drop-out, who had been in hassle with the law. They moved to Myrtle Beach to live in a cramped trailer with his circle of relatives. The boy worked production off and on, not an activity that would circulate Ella out of the poverty she knew so properly. Later in the year, she had a baby female. She named her Abra. To the question of why that unusual name, Ella might respond, "It became my pal's call. My best friend." Ella changed into doomed to maintain the existence of hopelessness that her circle of relatives had recognized for generations, but perhaps she had goals for her daughter. Maybe her Abra might make a hit break out.

Abra couldn't accept it as true with the sight earlier than her eyes. Pete drove up in the same Jeep he had for at least twenty years. She threw her suitcase in the again and hugged him tightly. It changed so correctly to peer this Viking who changed into still good-looking despite his thinning hair and sprouting potbelly. Abra spread out with "You still have this demise lure"

"I wouldn't give my cherished Jeep up even though I was presented 1,000,000 bucks. Well, perhaps a million, however not a half million. I idea you'd enjoy being in this because it brings again such a lot of satisfied recollections." They drove over the clunky, historical bridge to Mount Pleasant and then the older, clunkier draw bridge to Sullivan Island. Abra continually feared the teetering, creaking bridges from Charleston, however, something turned on the other facet made the white knuckle pressure worth it.

Before they drove to the residence, Pete drove past the cottage where Abra and Judy had lived. The Nelsons had constant it up and sold it for considerable earnings. It didn't appear to be an equal residence, it become converted with new shingles, brilliant paint, and landscaping. But the reminiscences of that house remained and most of the reminiscences were of Judy. Although Abra and Judy had lived collectively for three years in Grad College that they had now not been near. They shared instructions and went out collectively with their school buddies. Most in their lives were focused on getting to know their career. But that was modified in that residence on Sullivan Island. They have become buddies throughout racial strains, something neither had ever skilled before.

Growing up in a Jewish ghetto in Queens and going to a white school in Virginia, Abra had little touch with blacks. Judy had grown up having little touch with whites, living within the South facet black ghetto of Chicago and going to all black simple and secondary schools. Her mom turned into a single parent operating two jobs to assist Judy who attended the University of Illinois at Chicago, her first revel in an integrated college placing. She graduated with a 3.08 GPA and got an assistantship at USC for the graduate psych software. In Columbia, Judy straddled lives. She changed into a part of the mainly white global graduate faculty and lifestyles with white Abra. But she found a brand new black world of nicely knowledgeable people who also went to and fro from white to black. For the primary time, she dated white guys. She had never been inquisitive about white men but discovered that many were interested in her honey pores and skin, uncontrollable bush of kinky hair reluctantly pulled tight in a ponytail, and skinny discern accentuated by way of a sticking out butt.

During their twelve months in Charleston, Abra and Judy bonded, in element because they didn't have time for every person or anything aside from work. Walks at the seashore were the settings for many conversations on race and identification and dreams. Abra didn't sense any identity troubles due to being Jewish, possibly because she wasn't non secular. Her emotions of being one of a kind had been primarily based on being from a loveless, dysfunctional home. However, she found out about the tribulations of being black from Judy's descriptions of her college students' lives. Abra labored in a predominantly white, center magnificence school whilst Judy worked in a very black, poor, internal town faculty. Although the schools had been just a few miles apart bodily, they have been continents aside educationally and socially. They contrasted the lives of their students, every mastering from the alternative. They witnessed how race and social magnificence played out in the colleges. Although Ella was white, she shared a few of the overwhelming problems of blacks, especially generational poverty, the foundation of a lot of the evil they saw in their students' lives.

Abra additionally found out from Judy about a court that turned completely alien to her, passionate mom-daughter love. Adoring, selfless mother love was something Abra had most effectively read approximately, however, now she witnessed it first-hand. Over their year together, Judy described how her mom, Gale, committed her life to make it feasible for Judy to realize her desires There changed into no sacrifice Gale wouldn't make for her Judy.

Gale married Marlin, an immigrant from Jamaica who worked jobs to help his wife and newborn daughter. One night time coming home from his second task as a dishwasher in an upscale downtown Chicago eating place, he was mugged. He became shot useless for the ten dollars in his wallet. Judy was eighteen months old. She had no reminiscences of her father. She had handiest her mom's memories of a warm, loving own family man and a few pics of a smiling light-skinned guy with a head of kinky hair just like Judy's, During the day, Gale labored as a nurse's aide at the University of Chicago hospital and at night time she child sat with kids whose mothers labored night jobs. There have been always children snoozing on Gale's mattress and another on a cot, at the same time as Gale slept on the sofa. She didn't want to paint at night due to the fact she didn't need to be far away from Judy and she turned afraid to be out at night time. The reminiscence of Marlin being shot as he walked domestic from the bus haunted her on every occasion she changed into out after dark.

Gale changed into Judy's Miss Benjamin, however greater. Gale constantly stated, "You can do something on this global. You have the brains and the desire. I'll do whatever I can to make you the big name I recognize you may be. You are excellent!" Over and over Judy heard those phrases and she absorbed them, understanding her goals have been viable. As Judy grew, she dreamed of turning into an attorney and having her mother live together with her for the rest of her existence so she wouldn't have to paint. Judy didn't end up a lawyer, however, she did end up a psychologist and her mother did stay with her for the rest of her life.

Abra had never recognized a person who had misplaced a cherished one to homicide. This kind of violence become what she saw on TV, but to realize a person who turned into a sufferer turned horrifying. Judy pointed out the inner metropolis children she labored with who knew murder on each day foundation. Murder changed into within the streets and in the houses in which bullets have been randomly fired into houses killing harmless kids looking at TV or mothers nursing their babies. This became an international that Abra should handiest see via Judy's eyes. The children in Abra's college were concerned about a few violence at home or with gangs, however, by no means did this random mayhem victimize the black community. They did now not stay in a country of perpetual fear of being killed for no motive.

Abra and Judy's courting became capped through the graduation ceremony once they were given their doctorates. Neither Abra nor Judy cared a good deal about going to the commencement, but they knew that Miss Benjamin and Gale needed to see the fruits of their years of support and love. On a sweltering day in Columbia, Abra have become Dr. Berg and Judy have become Dr. Hurley. Miss Benjamin and Gale cheered loudly as their women obtained their hoods. They spent an entire afternoon in a cold air-conditioned eating place reminiscing approximately the past five years and questioning their futures, Abra working as a college psychologist and Judy coaching in the psychology department at a state university in Illinois. Both Miss Benjamin and Mrs. Hurley glowed with pleasure at the completed products they helped mold. Abra and Judy overflowed with gratitude for having such loving folks that made their goals. The two older girls used Dr. Berg and Dr. Hurley throughout the afternoon. "Pass the salt, Dr. Berg…Dr. Hurley, do you want to order a few desserts now?"

Abra ordered wine for all and sundry so that she may want to talk about her emotions via toasts. Abra raised her glass and as she regarded from Miss Benjamin to Mrs. Hurley, she stated, "To of the finest girls who ever lived. Two of the maximum unselfish ladies in the world. To the true heroines of existence – Edith Benjamin and Gale Hurley."

Abra and Judy had simplest visible each other three instances account that commencement, two times at psych conventions, and once at Judy's wedding two years after they graduated. Judy had fallen in love with Harold, a geology professor at the college where she become teaching. The reality that Harold turned into Jamaican like her father was a plus. Judy requested Abra to be her maid of honor and Abra proudly general. This turned into her second time as maid of honor, the primary at Beth and Tom's huge church wedding in Richmond. This wedding ceremony become small with simplest Mrs. Hurley, Harold's mother and father from Jamaica, and a few pals that they had made at the college. They were married in the university chapel and had a champagne brunch at a nearby outdoor eating place. It became an excellent day for Judy. All her desires had been found out – a doctorate, a university coaching task, and a splendid husband. Two years later they moved to a university in California and twelve months after that Judy had an infant boy, named Marlin. Her mother moved to California to take care of the infant at the same time as Judy persevered operating. Abra kept promising to visit them but had not gotten round to it yet. Maybe at some point. She did need to look for another happy family, particularly for someone who so deserved happiness. Judy had realized the American dream that turned unbelievable to her black ancestors who have been dragged onto Sullivan Island soil masses of years in the past. Her breakout became made feasible by a selfless, loving mother.

Abra checked out the Nelson residence – it had a sparkling coat of paint and a brand new roof, however, it still changed into the welcoming haven from seven years in the past. As Abra entered the front door, Martha ran into her fingers. They hugged for a long time, just savoring every different presence.

Martha said: "Before we start speaking and talking, permit us to eat. Everything is prepared to be wolfed." Martha had usually been a great cook dinner. She believed that cooking was a creative art similar to portraying and performing. Abra had never been capable of expanding a hobby in cooking, it became simply something you did so you didn't eat TV dinners all of the time.

Martha made an egg/cheese casserole, blueberry desserts, homemade strawberry preserves, and delicious robust espresso. The first time Abra had eaten desserts and preserves that Martha made from scratch, she changed into dumbfounded. How did human beings get the time to try this? Where did they get the components? Martha didn't even comply with recipes. How did she recognize what to apply and how much? Was this a few sorts of inborn talent, like the best pitch? They ate breakfast, wiped clean up, and which headed to the seaside with the dogs. Abra took off her footwear and walked inside the wet sand savoring the feel of the corporation and but tender, transferring sand. Pete walked off with the dogs as he threw sticks for them to fetch. Martha and Abra sat on straw mats maintaining arms and watching Pete, the puppies, and the sea.

Abra's plan no longer to tell Martha about her circle of relatives dissolved as soon as Abra opened her mouth. She needed to confess to Martha mainly, after wondering lower back to Ella. She used the same words that she had used with Beth the day earlier. This become going to be her canned speech recited in an equal manner as she made her confession to increasingly more people.

"Martha, I need to inform you about my secrets and techniques. You've usually recognized that I harbored plenty of secrets and techniques and you've never asked." She started with seeing the newspaper article at National Airport and ended with coming to Charleston an afternoon overdue.

When she completed, Martha stated, "I'm so glad you told me. It places loads of things into an angle." She tightly squeezed Abra's hand. "Are you amazed approximately my own family?"

"No. I knew they weren't useless however I had no idea you had siblings. When you came to my residence after the incident with Ella, you said things that made me suspect that they were alive. You're probable now not even privy to what you said. You were in the sort of distraught state. You pointed out all of the matters that Ella ought to do if she ran away. It turned obvious you were thru this yourself. You supplied an excessive amount of elements for this to have been a spur-of-the-moment analysis. I became tempted to project you, but it wasn't the proper time and it by no means become after that. I knew that one day you'd inform me of the truth. But really, I'm shocked with the aid of your family. You have this type of sharp thought. It's hard to imagine you coming from a circle of relatives of constrained intelligence. Pete and I notion that you in all likelihood came from a properly educated, intellectual own family and that you were abused or there was some trauma in the circle of relatives that drove you away. Other than the incident with Ella, you continually were on top of things and seemed to have a lot of power, but perhaps not. Maybe there's nonetheless an infant interior you desire to be nurtured. You in no way did have adolescence. You have been a person when you need to had been taking piano classes and going to Girls Scouts and sitting on your dad's lap hearing testimonies approximately his desires for you. You overlooked a variety of lifestyles. Maybe that's why you always had a certain expression on your face once I'd see you staring intently at my children. I think it became envy. You desired formative years like they were having and also you knew that would never appear. Or perhaps you had been sending them a silent message that they have been so lucky to have a loving own family, something that turned into denied you."

As Abra sobbed, she said, "I concept I changed into so appropriate at covering my past, however glaringly no longer since you and Beth both knew. But you had been both so true no longer to make me inform you till you knew I changed into ready. And now I'm equipped even though I have to admit not willingly, most effective because I should. I hate for people to realize my beyond. I need to simplest be Abra Berg, no longer Abra Ginzberg."

"But you'll always be Abra Ginzberg. You can't make her

depart. She'll continually be there inner you. You have to discover ways to build on her, now not cowl her up."

Pete came back with the dogs and knew that he had ignored something significant, however, he additionally knew that Martha could proportion all with him later. "We'd higher pass fast otherwise you're going to overlook your plane. Let's de-seaside and get transferring."

They went again to the residence for a wash-up and then drove to the airport. She hugged every one of them closely and stated to Martha, "I wish we had more time to talk. I constantly feel cleansed once I've talked with you. Please e-mail me or call me as you think about what I've told you. I need your mind. I want your know-how."

"I'll be in contact. I'm your buddy and continually can be. Come again at Christmas whilst the children are right here." "I'll be lower back."